Avalon Summer

JENNIFER M. BALDWIN

Printed in the United States of America
Published in 2023 by Phoenix and Fox Emporium
First paperback edition, 2023

Phoenix and Fox Emporium
www.phoenixandfoxemporium.com

Avalon Summer/Jennifer M. Baldwin — 1st ed.
Paperback ISBN: 978-1-959362-03-6

Contents

For my family

Preface

If I could name one literary inspiration for this novel, it would be Ray Bradbury's *Dandelion Wine*.

When I first read *Dandelion Wine*, I wasn't sure what to expect. It wasn't like *Fahrenheit 451* or *The Martian Chronicles*, the two other Bradbury novels I'd read. It was like tasting summer for the first time, like reliving my own childhood, even though Bradbury's childhood was nearly seventy years before mine.

Dandelion Wine captured something of what it means to be a wide-eyed kid, growing up in the Midwest, finding wonders in the everyday occurrences of life, seeing the magic in simple rituals of family and community.

Reading *Dandelion Wine* made me want to write something similar about my own childhood.

It may not have been the summer of '28, but the summer of '92 was a pivotal one for me. I was turning eleven, getting ready to start middle school, and finding that I had to make a choice about who I wanted to be: Was I going to keep playing make-believe, running through the woods pretending to be one of King Arthur's knights? Or was I going to put all that "nerdy stuff" behind me and strive for "popularity" and "coolness" and all the other things pre-teens are supposed to strive for?

The 1990s were a different time. Fantasy wasn't yet mainstream. There was no Peter Jackson's *Lord of the Rings*, no *Game of Thrones* TV series, no *Harry Potter*. In the early '90s, fantasy was not cool.

But looking back at my imaginary adventures, with the hindsight of adulthood and (I hope) some measure of wisdom, I can see how wrong I was about what's cool and what's not. I wish I could go back and visit my ten-year-old self and tell her to keep reading those fantasy paperbacks, to keep rolling those twenty-sided dice, to keep seeing ogres in the forest and running off to fight them.

Avalon Summer is my attempt at a 1990s version of *Dandelion Wine*. I make absolutely no secret about that. I know it's not nearly as good as Bradbury's classic, but I hope in some small way it gives homage to it. I wear my influences on my sleeve. Maybe it's not cool or popular, but I can't help it. I'm old enough now to not care what people will say.

Avalon Summer

CHAPTER ONE

Summer 1992

June 15th. 1992. The first official day of summer vacation.

Sky pale, early morning dew still fresh on the grass, and shadows from the nearby woods, still deep and black, gathering like an encroaching darkness over the sleeping world.

Soon the sun would pierce the shadows, send them scurrying, dry up the dew, and open the day to its endless possibilities. Soon the tang of adventure would drip off oak leaf and maple bark, would cascade through bedroom windows and front doors, would burst out of lawn sprinklers and squirt guns and soak the imaginations of every kid in the neighborhood.

Sarah Lewis, almost eleven, felt the brightness of the risen June sun against her eyelids. She didn't open them at first, even though she was awake. She wanted to savor the moment.

This was a summer that would promise magic, enchanted places, great battles against evil, great quests for heroes. There would be sword fights and monster hunts and ghosts-in-the-graveyard games. There would be sleepovers, board games, video game tournaments. There would be movies and swimming and Chinese take-out on Saturday nights, and bike rides. There would be books too. Sarah had stacked them next to her bed—the books of summer—and more would come soon. That was one of the first things. A visit to the Book Depot. Sarah would have her books, and she would read them all before summer's end, a mountain of dreams and dragons.

She would have her sword too. Grandpa Ray had promised. A blade of balsam wood. Alex wanted one too. Together they'd swing swords at trees and call them ogres.

Sarah opened her eyes. She gazed at the fat spines of her tower of books. She glanced out her window and saw nothing but green: the swaying leaves of a thousand trees.

She smiled.

Fried eggs and sausage wafted up the stairs, trickled their scent under her bedroom door. She jumped out of bed and greeted the morning, the beginning of her best summer ever.

CHAPTER TWO

The Rusted Gates of Avalon

THE WOODS SHIVERED and lurched from side to side. The branches shook their leaves, rattled their bones.

The wind felt good in the hotness of the heavy thicket.

"Avalon is ruled by nine queens. They rule it with terrible magic." Sarah trudged through a sea of brown leaves, her knobby knees smudged by dirt and nicked by scratches from thorny brambles. She pushed a strand of brown hair behind her ear, a nervous habit.

Alex followed. "What's the magic do?" His dark eyes were like shining marbles peering out from his coffee-colored skin.

"Puts people to sleep. Does enchantments and stuff. It's powerful."

"So we have to fight the witches?"

"The queens."

"Okay, queens." Alex looked up above the shaking trees and caught flashes of blue sky, his narrow chin jutting out with slight defiance.

"We have to save the knight. The Oak-Hearted Knight." Sarah pushed back branches, bounded over tree trunks.

"He's got an oak heart?"

"No, it just means he's, like, good and stuff. He's strong and helps his friends."

"Okay…"

Alex made a face, but Sarah didn't see. She was resolute, quixotic. She marched through the woods with one purpose, one mission: the gates.

"Anyway," she continued, "he went to Avalon to find his lady love, and the queens trapped him in a magic sleep."

"That's it? We have to wake up some dude?"

"That's not it!" Sarah stopped and swung herself around to face him. "We have to break the enchantment!" Her eyes flashed, her heart beat faster. She had to make him see that this quest was worthy of their summer, that it was something special. "And that means fighting the nine queens. Each one has a different magic, and they want to trap us too. Keep us forever in Avalon."

"Okay, fine, but how do we fight them? We don't even have swords."

Sarah knew his frustration. She longed for a sword too. "We'll get swords. My grandpa said he'd make them."

"Yeah, but he hasn't yet. Let's just go back and go swimming. I'm hot."

The heat was measurable by the number of bees that swarmed through the woods. With every step into the heart of the forest, their numbers increased tenfold. Sarah bit her lip and tried not to see the bees or feel their buzzing against her neck.

"Is this all a story from a book?" Alex asked.

"No," Sarah answered, "not yet."

"Look!" Alex pointed across the creek.

They had been following the banks of the water since they

came into the woods. Now they met the bridge that would take them across.

An old oak had fallen: wayward soul, unadmired lord of the forest. It had lain itself across the waters of the creek. A tree bridge to carry them on their quest.

A beehive hung low in an ash tree on the other side.

The bees came in and out of the hive, a dozen at a time.

"Let's go back," said Alex.

Sarah put her foot on the tree bridge. "We're doing this."

Inching forward, tennis shoes met with slick moss. Bark flaked off with each footfall. The creek below ate the pieces, gushing in a torrent of brown silt and algae, crashing through the silence like a thunderstorm.

The bees were the only other sound, buzzing like saw-blades thirsty for skin. Sarah's skin prickled, and the heat flushed to her face. Bees surrounded her. Her feet moved unconsciously across the log. She floated. She walked the tightrope. Tennis shoes at last met heavy, sodden earth. She almost fell to her knees when she made it across.

Instead, she stared at the beehive, hypnotized by the swarm, waiting for their stingers, wondering if she would die.

"Go, go!" Alex shouted from halfway across the bridge. He barreled forward. Sarah ran, brushing past the beehive and the ash tree and galloping up the hill beyond.

Alex followed her, close on her heels, and the buzzing of the bees faded, mingled with the echoing sounds of the creek, until they were at the top of the hill and the silence of the sun was the only thing they could hear. And the trees were thinner. A clearing up ahead. Almost like someone's backyard lawn. The musty leaves of the forest floor were gone. Disappeared. Brambles too. Replaced by sunshine and green grass and open air. But it was no backyard, just a clearing: an empty, flat, unremarkable clearing.

And in the center of it were the gates.

Cold and iron, dark as shadows, they were shut and locked, two heavy, silent sentinels that guarded no one and enclosed nothing. They weren't attached to any wall, they didn't block any path. They simply rested in the middle of the clearing, sprouted up from the ground like a line of weeds. Wrought iron and ancient-looking, they made no sense. Just a pair of gates for a house unbuilt, for a park unfinished, for a property unclaimed. Or they were made by fairy hands. Or by witches.

"It's the only way to Avalon," Sarah whispered.

Alex didn't care about the silence or the solemnity of the place. He marched up to the gates and rattled them.

"Locked," he said. He turned back to Sarah. "I don't get it. Are we supposed to open them? Why not just go around?"

"That's not the point."

"What do they do? Take us to this other place?"

"To Avalon."

"Good, let's go."

Sarah had the key out of her pocket before she even knew it.

"A skeleton key!" Alex leaned in. He gaped at the strange object.

Sarah held it like a relic, something holy, something true. It burned with unseen fire, but Sarah held it fast. It was the first piece of magic she'd ever held.

"I found it in my grandpa's garage. Just lying there in the bottom of his toolbox."

"But it can't work, can it?"

It would. Sarah knew it.

But when she pushed the key into the lock something stopped her from turning it. She looked back, saw Alex's face, saw the sun shining high in the empty blueness of mid-June. The heat from the sun was too hot, the woods too full of afternoon insects. And Alex's face was too unbelieving. He looked at Sarah and the gates as if they were nothing more than a game, like freeze tag or hide-and-go-seek or ghosts-in-the-graveyard. Somewhere, far off in the subdivision up the hill, past the woods, a garage door clanked open and drew with it the faint sound of car doors opening and shutting. The sun was a spotlight now, a glaring voyeur, an unkind face. The trees around the clearing swayed, their leaves humming with a warning.

"We can't go in," she said, taking the key out of the lock. "It's the wrong time."

"Wrong time? No way, Sarah! We're not leaving without going through. We came all the way here."

"We can't." She turned her back on the gates. "Gotta be at dusk. The key doesn't work without the moon and the sun both in the sky."

"You just made that up."

"Did not."

"You did, and this game is stupid."

Sarah didn't answer. She knew Alex was wrong, but she couldn't explain why. The gates were real. Avalon was real. She knew it had to be.

"Fine," she said, putting the key back in her pocket. "Let's go swimming."

"Or play space army?" Alex was eager.

"Fine, I'll play space army with you."

Alex straightened his shoulders and took charge. "We're using guns."

"Fine."

Neon-colored squirt guns sprinkled the grass with misty streams of water. Vast alien races fell beneath the onslaught. Alex stood triumphant upon the bricks of Grandpa Ray's fire pit, while Sarah's eyes flitted every so often toward the edge of the woods. She thought she heard the buzzing of bees.

Somewhere, in that vast deepness of greens and browns and dark shade, the gates waited and kept watch. The skeleton key rattled in Sarah's pocket. It almost whispered to her, and she watched as the sun fell lower in the sky and dusk made its slow creep into the world.

The space victory had been won. Alex wiped sweat and cold water from his brow and a bright grin peeled its way over his lips. He looked up toward the black and white house on the hill, saw the place where his bike rested against the garage wall, let his squirt gun drop to his side.

"Gotta go," he said, then rushed up the hill in a mad, breakneck sprint.

Sarah followed, legs charging, but her heart seized up. Her lungs tightened. She felt the sting of regret.

She told herself: There would be another dusk, another chance. The gates would wait, the magic would hold. But still, she swallowed her regret.

Bats flitted above them in the tree tops, and soon Alex's feet found the pedals of his bike. Sarah waved as he peeled away down the long asphalt driveway. Dreaming of ancient queens and sleeping warriors, Sarah ran in the opposite direction. The skeleton key rattled in her pocket, and then the screen door banged shut as she let it fly.

Grandma and Grandpa were already on the living room couch watching an old black and white Sherlock Holmes movie with Basil Rathbone. Grandpa had his bowl of popcorn resting on his lap. Grandma snored a little.

Sarah ran upstairs to her bedroom and shut the door. The room was empty; her brother must've been playing his video games in the spare room. She sat on her bed and caught her breath. Outside, through her window, she could still see the trees of the surrounding woods, darkened and forbidding. The fireflies had come out and danced on the lawn. She sat on her bed for a long time, holding the skeleton key in the palm of her hand.

The gates would wait. And she would be ready.

CHAPTER THREE

The Bats

THE KIDS DECIDED it would be fun to swim at night. Even though the sun had started to drop toward the horizon, the water was warmer at dusk. The looming trunks of the surrounding trees became thick black lines that sliced their way down the orange sky.

Alex swam laps deep below the surface, gliding through the water like an eel. Sarah floated on her back and watched the clouds disappear into the growing darkness of the sky. Blue faded imperceptibly into black. They got out onto the deck a few times and cannonballed into the water. The air was tinged with an evening chill, but the water got warmer and warmer with each jump.

It was 8:30 p.m., June 17. The bats had just started to rise from their tree-top beds. They lingered in the woods around the Ray house. They hadn't ventured forth.

Grandpa Ray came outside. He was wearing his dark blue silk pajamas.

"You kids gonna lock up," he said. It was not a question. It was a statement of absolute, irrefutable fact. "Make sure to put the chlorine in."

Then he was gone, back to the house to watch some *Perry Mason* and eat his nightly bowl of popcorn.

Sarah kept floating as she stared up at the sky. Alex kept his nose just above the surface of the water and lurked like some kind of insidious frog. It was warmer to stay as fully submerged as possible. The twilight air was sunless now.

The bats came out.

Sarah thought they were birds at first. She let them fly and flit above her. Then two of them dipped low, close to the top of the pool deck, and something about the way their wings fluttered, the violent way they jerked and changed direction in the sky made Sarah suddenly jump. She let herself sink into the placid water, her mouth just barely hovering above the surface. She crept as low as she could without going under. She tried to escape the bats.

"Bats!" cried Alex. The creatures had a different effect on him. He jumped up from his low position in the water and stood flatfooted at the bottom of the pool. He wanted to be closer to the night flyers. He braved the coldness of the air as it prickled his skin. The bats swooped and danced, coming ever lower, hunting bugs unseen. Alex tried to keep track of each one as it passed overhead. Sarah kept herself hidden in the inky waters.

Night was rushing into the woods and the sprawling yard and the pool and the glowing house nearby.

A voice broke the darkness. It stung with sour petulance. "Skinning dipping with your girlfriend? Oh, wait. You're too much of a pussy!" The voice laughed.

Alex's older brother Julian skidded the tires of his bike on the asphalt. He stood straddling the bike on the long driveway that ran next to the swimming pool. He glared up through the wooden fencing on the deck, trying to find

Alex's brown skin in the darkness. His face perpetually sneered.

"Let's go, jackwad. Dad says you gotta come home. Doesn't want you out past dark."

Alex didn't get out of the pool. He watched the bats swoop lower and lower.

"Whatever," Julian shrugged. "Have fun riding home in the dark."

Alex smiled as the bats chased their prey across the lawn. A dozen of them danced now, catching mosquitoes, devouring the moths and bloodsuckers that swarmed over the grass. He watched as they flew in manic circles over and around and under tree limbs. He watched as they drifted and danced toward the long driveway as if to follow Julian on his bike. Julian pedaled hard, happy to leave his brother to fend for himself. The bats followed their prey.

Sarah stayed mostly submerged. A few stragglers still flitted close above them in the pool. Alex stretched out his arms as if he hoped one of the bats would alight on his sprawling fingers. None did.

"I guess I better go," he said.

Everything was darkness now. The wood of the deck, the trees surrounding them, the basketball pole, Grandma's car parked in the driveway: Everything was covered in blackness, everything a formless suggestion in the shadowed night. The water was the only thing that contained any light, but it was a dull light, faintly green, a reflection of the green laminate that covered the walls and floor of the pool.

Alex climbed up the ladder and onto the deck. He wiped the chilled water off his skin, hung his towel over the fencing around the deck, and bounded down the steps to the asphalt below. Sarah stayed hidden in the water. She kept her eyes fixed above, scanning for bats.

Alex put his t-shirt on and straddle his bike. "Thanks!" he grinned, invisible in the darkness.

Sarah said nothing, her words catching in her throat. She remembered that her grandpa had asked her to put chlorine in the pool. The thought of walking between the shed and the pool, alone in the darkness, kept her body safely in the water. She would have to walk all the way around—high on the edge of the deck—and drop the chemicals into the water. She would have to put herself closer to the bats.

"Bye," she managed, too softly, as Alex rode off. She scanned the sky above for sight of the creatures. She lingered in the water. Mosquitoes started to gnaw at her face.

ALEX PEDALED DOWN THE DRIVEWAY, between the trees on either side, his wet hair whipping in the wind, his t-shirt billowing behind him. He felt unfettered. Julian had tried to taunt him, frighten him with being alone, but he reveled in his aloneness. The bats beat their wings above him, riding with him through the night. He saw streaks of fireflies on either side, but he was the night air and the cool wind and he flew. He did not stop to see if opossums or deer were gazing at him from the depths of the wilderness. He rode over smooth asphalt, he closed his eyes and sensed only the air and the weightlessness of his flight. The bats streaked from bough to bough above his head. They tasted the mosquitoes and the cool June air. Alex thought he could almost taste the sharp metallic flavor of blood. Julian would never have dared such freedom.

Alex broke out into the open of the subdivision, leaving the cavern of trees behind. As he pulled into his own driveway, heading for the garage, the bats left him. They soared and disappeared into the night clouds and headed back to their feast on the lawn of the Rays' endless yard. Alex was human again. But his eyes blinked twice—startled and uneasy —as they met the yellow light that had been left on for him in the kitchen.

IN THE RAY HOUSE, Sarah sneaked in past her sleeping grandparents and scurried up to her bedroom. The chlorine powder in the shed lay untouched.

The bats, turning in circles above the water, danced.

CHAPTER FOUR

The Headstone

"IT'S A GRAVESTONE," Julian said. His mouth twisted into an ugly smile. "It's even got a date."

It was true. The stone had "1905" chiseled into it.

"Eighty-six years ago," Jay said.

Julian snickered. "What are you, some kind of human computer?" he said.

Sarah shivered at the thought of someone buried under the ground where they all stood. Someone buried so long ago. She could feel the eyes of ghosts peering at her from behind every tree in the woods. They were out of sight of her grandparents' house, deep in the forest. She thought of the queens of Avalon, of their dark magic, of their shadowy forms winding through the trees, looking for prey.

What if the queens killed this person? she thought. What if they killed anyone who got too close to the gates? She looked around again and thought she saw something move nearby. She stepped closer to her brother, but Jay took no notice of her nerves.

"But no name," Jaime said, his voice coated in skepticism. He swept the hair out of his eyes, a habit intended to make himself look cool. Jaime was a bit pudgier than Julian, so he made sure to always have the perfect haircut and the perfect outfit too in order to outdo his younger brother. Right now he was wearing a leather belt and nice, new Birkenstocks. Julian was wearing ratty sneakers and a faded Guns 'n' Roses shirt. Sarah's brother, Jay, looked the most pedestrian of the three: basketball shorts that hung to his knees, an old t-shirt, hair buzzed short.

While Julian scowled, Jaime let loose his lazy, half-crooked smile. Sarah thought it made him look much friendlier.

"It could also be a plaque or something. Like, maybe a house was built here," Jaime continued.

"This is the edge of a freakin' hill, ass," responded Julian. "What idiot builds a house here? The whole thing would be slanted."

Sarah wasn't quite sure that Julian's logic made sense. Building a house at the top of a hill was probably a good idea; after all, Grandpa Ray's house was at the top of a hill. Of course, she preferred Jaime's theory anyway. Better to think a house once stood here than to think they were trespassing on a grave. She eyed the trees again for some sign of the Avalon queens.

Jay knelt and started to lift the heavy slab off the ground.

"Jay, stop!" Sarah panicked when she saw his fingers curl under the stone. She stepped back with a jerk and almost lost her footing down the side of the hill.

Jay heaved the heavy concrete stone up and dumped it over so that the engraved date now lay face-down in the dirt. There was a heavy, rectangular impression in the wet earth where the slab had been.

And bones.

Sarah swallowed her scream. She stepped back even

further, this time making sure to watch her footing. She looked around at the silent trees and mistook every squirrel for a vengeful specter or a witch.

The boys, on the other hand, crowded around the bones.

"Animal," Jaime said with a tinge of smugness. "Probably a squirrel or something."

"But they're too big to be a squirrel," replied Jay. "Look, buried there." He reached down and dug at the dirt around what looked like a jawbone. As his fingers cleared the dirt away, they could see the skull of the creature more clearly.

"It's way bigger than a squirrel," Jay continued. "And look at the teeth."

Julian smirked. "I know what it is." He paused for effect, but it only seemed to work on Sarah. She felt her stomach grow tight. She had no idea why the thought of an animal being buried there filled her with dread, but the hairs on the back of her neck prickled.

The other two boys didn't seem to care.

"It's a fox," Julian finished.

His words failed to impress Jaime or Jay.

"Yeah, I can see that," said Jaime. "But why the hell would someone put a grave marker for a dead fox? It's just a coincidence."

"Lame!" Julian snapped. "Let's get out of here."

The older boys got on their bikes and started peddling down the dirt path in the woods that led back to Grandpa Ray's property.

Sarah stood looking at the fox bones. She wished Alex was there. He was at his piano lessons, leaving Sarah on her own. She felt as if at any moment, the queens of Avalon were going to appear from behind the trees and offer her up as a sacrifice.

She screwed up her courage and knelt closer to the fox

bones. She tried to imagine that they had once been covered by skin and fur. She tried to imagine them moving, padding through the leaves and twigs of the forest.

But all she saw were bones.

Using every bit of her strength, Sarah pushed the headstone onto its edge and then let it drop with a heavy thud on top of the bones. They rested in peace again.

She didn't go back to her grandparents' house. She wandered the woods, climbing higher and higher up the hills that led to property that went beyond what Grandpa Ray owned. There was a silent yellow field of dried wheat beyond the woods. It seemed like a place of ghosts to Sarah. She and Alex had glimpsed it before, traipsing along the edge of the woods, telling tales of goblins and dragons in the forest. But now Sarah headed straight for the field.

Resting like a sleeping giant, a faded red barn stood brooding over the deserted field. Its walls were somehow held together at slanted angles. Shadows cut through the broken slats of the wooden beams. It was all bones, no flesh. Next to the barn sat a barrel filled with sludgy, stagnant rainwater. Farm tools rusted in the hot sunlight, abandoned decades ago; they were things Sarah could not name, strange tools that seemed more suited to a medieval dungeon than to a deserted farm.

She crept nearer and nearer to the barn. She wasn't sure why or what she was looking for. Maybe she wanted to find the spirit of the fox. All she knew as she stepped into the hot noon sunshine was that this field and this barn were not part of the same world as the forest. The forest was a bridge, a between-world, a passageway to realms of Faerie and enchanted kingdoms. But this field and this dead farm were frighteningly real. They were part of the haunted past, the same as the fox. They were tangible ghosts.

A wild thought flew into Sarah's mind: She was going to go into the barn. Something lived there, and it was different from the iron gates of Avalon or the stories of the Oak-Hearted Knight and the queens. Inside that barn was a real adventure. Real danger.

Dragonflies rocketed around the barrel of black water, landing sometimes on the edge of the wooden rim, other times speeding around the rusted tools which lay strewn about the dried grass. Sarah watched her step as she pushed through the tall grass, keeping an eye out for snakes or mice. The silence was broken only by an eerie humming that came from every direction.

She realized suddenly that she was totally alone. Her stomach leaped into her throat. She peered into the darkness of the broken barn. There wasn't enough light to see anything but shadows; there weren't enough broken beams to see anything but more darkness.

I'll have to go in, she thought.

Something moved inside the barn. Sarah knew it. For the briefest of moments, she wondered if it was a goblin, or a queen of Avalon. She felt the quickest half-heartbeat of a thrill, the thought soaring across her imagination like a sparrow in flight. The thrill was at once wonderful and dreadful. Magic was real. Something was inside the barn. A living thing, a wondrous thing.

Then the movement happened again, and as silly as it was, Sarah grew deeply frightened. She knew it wasn't a goblin, or a queen, or any kind of person at all. She knew in her heart that it was a raccoon. She could see its small, gleaming, beady eyes flash across the darkness at her. And in that instant, she was terrified of the raccoon. She was alone. The sun wasn't warm anymore; it was a searing blaze of terrible fire. It accused her of trespassing. She could feel its wrath igniting. The raccoons would soon swarm, no one would hear her, no one would know where she was.

She turned and ran. Gone were careful steps that looked for snakes and mice. Gone were any thoughts of adventure. She had trespassed on 1905, disturbed the bones of foxes and the residence of raccoons and real ghosts.

The fear lessened when she reached the dark shade of the woods, but she kept her feet from stopping. She sprinted. She flew through spindly branches and needled bushes. She burst out of the forest onto the long asphalt driveway that led up to Grandpa and Grandma Ray's house.

Her feet flapped down on the heavy pavement of the driveway, breaking the dreadful silence. The sun was her friend again. Behind her and to her right and left were the tall, leafy sentinels of the woods. The trees waved gently in their new-found breeze. They signaled to Sarah that they were hers again, her enchanted forest. She ran over the asphalt bridge that crossed the creek. The brown, slow-flowing water was her friend again too. She smiled.

The dead golden field and the ancient barn were gone, part of a dream that Sarah was already starting to forget. The barrel of rotten water was gone. The enemy eyes of raccoons were gone.

The huge black and white house on the hill smiled at her. Sarah ran along the stone-lined path. She flung open the screen door. She felt the cool rush of ceiling fans hit her face. She flopped down on the couch in the living room and turned on an old rerun, a garishly colored TV show from the 1960s, the kind that always got shown on a broadcast Tuesday afternoon, something to fill the empty airtime.

She sighed and breathed in the possibilities of summer, basking in the knowledge that the rest of the afternoon was hers and hers alone. She could watch TV or read a book or wait until Alex's piano lessons were over and invite him to go swimming. She didn't have to think about that field or the terrible rusted bones of ghosts. The possibilities of summer were a miracle that could cure any thought of fox bones or old barns. Sarah watched her TV show and let herself slip into such miracles.

CHAPTER FIVE

The Scarab Garden

THE MORNING WAS ALL GRAY. Sky was gray. Light was gray. Even the green grass in the yard, and the green grass that was poking its way through the garden, was gray. The grass was too long, growing up into wavy hairs that were weak and thin, and the grayness of the sky sifted through them and made the yellow-green blades grow dim.

Bud Henderson knew he needed to mow the lawn and weed the garden, but he puttered around amongst the cucumber plants instead. He wore a gray fishing hat, and light blue slacks, and his suspenders were once white but had grown grayer with time and use. Now they matched the color of his thinning hair. He watered the prickly vines of the cucumbers and counted the white and yellow blossoms that had sprouted.

The yard was quiet except for the occasional buzzing of cicadas and the flutter of dragonflies. A rather large bumblebee was surveying the flowers in the garden and lingering around Mr. Henderson's hat.

At the back of his yard was the woods. Henderson wasn't sure if he owned it or if it was part of the Rays' land.

Regardless, Joe Ray never bothered with the woods back there, and Mr. Henderson had his privacy.

The yard next door was another story. The boys lived there. The Guerrera boys. The two oldest, to be precise. Henderson was just about fed up with those boys, Julian and Jaime, always hitting baseballs into his yard and bulldozing through his garden. Mr. Henderson had spotted their footprints amongst his daisies. Carousers. Foul-mouthed. He wondered where their father was, and why the man couldn't control his offspring. Henderson would've had a paddle set aside for those two.

He sprinkled the last drops from his watering can onto the cucumbers. Then he jerked up with a start.

It was broken.

"Damned kids," he spat. He reached down and picked up the pieces of the broken amulet. It was cracked in half.

Someone had cracked it.

The break was too clean to have been an animal or an accident. It must have been intentional.

For twenty years, the black-colored scarab had rested in Bud Henderson's garden, a sacred, ancient guardian beneath the cucumbers and snap peas. It reminded him of Evie. He kept it in the garden as a tribute to her.

The name engraved on the stone in Egyptian hieroglyphics—Amunet—was now split in two. The name of the woman for whom the heart scarab had been made. The woman who had been buried with it.

Ah, Evie, so many years ago! What a time we had finding this one!

Bud blinked back tears. It felt wrong, somehow, to glue the pieces back together, but he couldn't stand to leave it broken. He cursed the Guerrera boys as he put the pieces in his pocket and felt the grayness of the backyard cover him like a shroud.

~

"Roll! It's your turn," Sarah said, practically flinging the dice at Alex. She was impatient for his turn to be over so she could claim the ruby jewel. One more move and it would be hers. She just knew it.

Alex rolled a one on the dice.

A red marble fireball (guided by Sarah's hand) promptly came lumbering down the plastic canal that led straight to Alex's game piece. The flimsy piece fell over and the red marble lolled from side to side next to it.

"Yes!" Sarah snatched up the dice and took command of the game. She rolled, and with her roll, claimed the ruby jewel that lay next to the black, demon-faced Tiki idol at the center of the 3-D game board. It took several rolls later to descend the jungle paths and reach the boat, but Sarah completed the quest.

"Play again?" she asked without taking a breath.

The sky was cloudy and beckoning rain. It had been a rainy few days.

Sarah and Alex sat at a white-painted picnic table under the aluminum awing that connected Grandpa Ray's house to his garage. It was the sort of dull day that kept even the bees and wasps inside their hives. "June Gloom," Sarah's mom, Anne, had called it. For Sarah, it was the perfect day to play board games.

Alex swung his legs over the picnic table bench and stood up. "We can ride to the bookstore and get some candy."

His bike was resting against the white stucco exterior of the garage. Sarah eyed it but didn't move from the table.

"What about the rain?" she asked.

But Alex just shrugged. "It's something to do."

"I guess."

They rode. The long driveway that stretched from the Rays' wooded property out to the subdivision was darker than usual. Without any sun to peak through, the woods and trees that loomed on either side of the asphalt made the driveway into a blackened tunnel. When they finally broke through into open air, the grayness in the sky was only a temporary relief.

"It's Mr. Henderson!" Alex cried as they drove past the elderly man's backyard.

Bud Henderson was still in his garden, puttering with the weeds.

"Hiya, Mr. Henderson!" Alex called, waving his hand to the hunched figure. Turning his bike from the asphalt to the grass, Alex rode over to Bud Henderson's yard.

Sarah hesitated, scanning the unmowed grass for Mr. Henderson's green-eyed tabby cat. Sarah was afraid of cats.

"Hello, Alex," Mr. Henderson said, straightening his back and letting out a sigh. His voice was gentle. Bud Henderson had no ill will toward the youngest Guerrera. Alex was a sweet boy with good manners.

"What'cha doing?" Alex asked, swinging his leg over the bike seat and putting the kickstand down.

Mr. Henderson let his lips curl into a slight smile. Alex was a good boy. Thoughtful.

The other two would've just let their bikes flop onto the grass.

"Weeding," answered the elderly man. "All that rain we've been having has made 'em sprout up. Tried to avoid it, but here I am."

Sarah parked her bike next to Alex's; she hadn't spotted the cat lurking anywhere.

Bud Henderson didn't know the Ray girl very well. She and her brother were visiting this summer, for the first time in years.

Though, I suppose she's not a Ray. She would have her mother's married name.

"Come in for a cup of iced tea?" Mr. Henderson asked, using his thick gardening gloves to wipe the dirt off his trowel.

Before Sarah could wonder if the cat lay waiting inside, Alex had chirped, "Sure!"

Mr. Henderson deposited his trowel and gloves in an old pot outside the back door and swung the screen door open.

The kitchen was laid out just like the one in the Guerrera house. Same linoleum table in the center, same arrangement of dark brown cupboards along the far wall, same yellow countertop that jutted out into the room.

What wasn't the same were the decorations.

Mr. Henderson's kitchen looked like the gift shop of an ancient history museum. Shriveled pieces of papyrus were encased on glass frames; the papyri were covered in tiny hieroglyphics and Sarah tried to make out what each picture might be, but she found her eyes wandering to the other treasures in the room. Shelves upon shelves were covered with bits of broken pottery and tiny bottles made of dark glass. The pieces of pottery were also covered in hieroglyphic symbols, while the dark glass seemed older than anything Sarah had ever seen. Stone tools, and even a few dull-looking daggers, hung from wall mounts, as did bejeweled disks of bronze, which shined like miniature suns, their metallic brightness contrasting with the brown wood paneling of the kitchen walls.

"Iced tea," Henderson said, pounding two glasses down on the linoleum table. Sarah picked up her glass but did not drink. Alex gulped down the tea heartily. Then his head tilted back a little and peeked out of the kitchen doorway into the living room just beyond.

"May I play the piano, Mr. Henderson?" Alex asked.

Mr. Henderson had his back to the children while he put the pitcher of iced tea back into the refrigerator. Without turning around he said, "Alright," and warned them not to take their drinks with them. "Those glasses stay in the kitchen," he said.

But when he turned around, Henderson was surprised to find the Ray girl still there, her unsipped iced tea in hand. Alex, in the other room, had already creaked open the cover of the piano and was noodling the keys.

"Go on," Henderson said to the girl. "Go with your friend."

Sarah hesitated. She didn't want to leave the kitchen; she was still mesmerized by the artifacts on the walls. But Mr. Henderson's glare was almost a scowl, and she didn't dare tempt him to throw her out or badger her for her rudeness. It seemed to Sarah that Mr. Henderson was just the type who would badger a kid for rudeness. She remembered to put her iced tea down, and then followed Alex into the living room.

Bud Henderson sat down at the kitchen table and sighed. He reached into his pocket and pulled out the two broken pieces of the scarab. The sound of Alex's playing lilted through the kitchen. Henderson had to admit, the young man was quite good. He played a few snippets of *Fir Elise* and then switched to a much harder concerto by Mozart.

"Well-mannered boy," Henderson said under his breath.

He turned the pieces of the scarab around in his hands. The break was smooth.

"Should be able to," he said to himself. He put the pieces down for a moment and got up to rummage through one of his junk drawers. Finding the bottle of glue, Henderson returned to the table and began to trace a small line of glue along the broken edge of one of the scarab pieces.

A shiver rose along his neck. Hand suddenly trembling, Henderson put the glue bottle down. He almost dropped the scarab piece too. Instead, he rested it gently on the linoleum and stared at the two broken pieces. A whisper crept along his skin. A voice. An echo.

"No," Henderson said, barely breathing. Both his hands were shaking now. At that moment, he realized the piano music had stopped.

He turned sharply. Both children were standing in the kitchen doorway, gaping at the scarab pieces.

"Cool!" Sarah said. "Is that thing an ancient treasure?"

She reached a hand toward the pieces, but Henderson slapped her fingers away. It was a harder slap than he intended.

The young girl's face was in shock as she rubbed her fingers.

Henderson's eyes seemed to burn in his skull—as if someone had lit them on fire—and his face twisted in rage.

Both Sarah and Alex backed away.

"Get out," Henderson said through clenched teeth.

Neither child hesitated. They scrambled for the back door that led out into the garden. Alex mumbled a sheepish apology as he left.

The screen door clanged shut like the snapping of a crocodile's jaws.

Bud Henderson was left alone.

The burning in his eyes had turned to tears. He blinked them back.

"Old fool," he mumbled to himself. He tried to forget that he had hit the young girl's hand.

"Kids," he said, shaking his head. The glue on the scarab pieces had been smudged. He went to get a wet cloth to wipe up the glue. After he cleaned the piece off, he tried again. He drew a thin line of glue on the broken edge of one of the pieces. Then, his hands still trembling, he tried to carefully place the two pieces back together. It took a few tries, but eventually, he managed to make the broken edges meet. He left the scarab on the kitchen table to let the glue dry.

Back in the garden, Henderson bent over the weeds and started to root them out. Despite the overcast sky and slight breeze, Bud Henderson started to sweat. A mugginess hung in the air as he worked. He felt his back creak as he shoved his trowel into the dirt and weeded out crabgrass and dandelions. He threw the weeds into a pile alongside the edge of his garden. At last, he felt his back twinge, and the sharp pain made him stand up to stretch.

A rustling noise came from the woods at the edge of his backyard. The branches of trees moved as if an animal was foraging there.

A large animal, Henderson thought. He peered into the thicket of brambles and tree branches. His yard stretched a long way back, making it hard to see much in the woods beyond.

He dropped his trowel. There was no mistaking it.

A woman stood hidden among the trees. She wore a gleaming necklace of jewels and jade that covered her chest and barely touched the tops of her breasts. Her skin was sun-touched, the color of autumn wheat. From the neck down, she was beautiful.

But it was not the woman's body that shocked Bud Henderson. It was her head.

Upon her long, delicate neck sat the head of a fearsome, bloodthirsty lion. The lion's eyes were narrowed, its prey sighted. Its lips curled slightly, showing the sharp gleam of its fangs.

Bud Henderson heard the lion growl.

The screen door slammed.

"Old fool!" Henderson spat, chiding himself. His breath was coming in great agonizing heaves, his chest tightening with each gasp. He needed to steady himself on the linoleum table.

The scarab sat on the table. It was broken in half again.

"Damned glue," Henderson mumbled between haggard breaths. He stumbled out of the kitchen and down the hallway toward his bedroom. When he reached his bedroom, he collapsed on the bed and tried to slow his breathing. He put his hand over his heart and could feel it beating so hard he worried it would pound right out of his chest.

He closed his eyes. The face of the lion woman flashed across the blackness in his mind, her eyes aglow with sun-like fire.

Henderson opened his eyes again and stared at the white ceiling. He turned his head and looked at the other side of the bed, the side where his wife used to sleep. The pillow was smooth, untouched, a cloud of crisp white floating on the crocheted blanket beneath. He let his hand wander across the blanket, tracing his fingers along the patterns of cornflowers and irises.

"Evie," he said softly.

He could see her now, long hair streaming out from under her hat as she stood next to the ruined tomb, the desert wind striking her face. Flecks of sand brushed her cheeks as the wind whirled past, but she just smiled defiantly. The sun had made her face ruddy and warm, her blue eyes piercing through the tanned skin. She was laughing; it was a fierce and free and unforgettable laugh.

Bud Henderson's breathing slowed. His heart returned to its normal pace. He remembered Evie laughing, her soft brown hair flying in the wind. He closed his eyes again and saw nothing but the dark behind his eyelids.

When he woke up, darkness had descended outside. Storm clouds had overruled the gray rain clouds from earlier, casting away all traces of light from the mid-afternoon sky. The rain was waiting to fall, the clouds pregnant with heavy droplets. Thunder shook the house and everything around it.

Henderson got up out of bed, his bones creaking from arthritis. He rubbed his eyes and tried to see in the darkness of the bedroom. He found the open door and went back down the hall to the kitchen, his dry throat thirsting for a glass of iced tea.

On the kitchen table, the scarab amulet was still broken in two. At first, Henderson ignored it. He poured his glass of iced tea and stood by the refrigerator drinking it. The cool, bitter tea coated his parched throat.

But the scarab found him, catching his eye the way a strange woman might catch one's eye in a crowded marketplace.

The rain broke. A sheet of water pounded down on the roof of the house. A flood poured over the garden outside.

Henderson looked out the kitchen window. His eyes only briefly glanced at the soaked garden and the tools he had dropped like stones in the muddy dirt; instead, they drifted with dreadful curiosity toward the woods beyond. It was too dark to see anything other than the green and brown outlines of leaves and limbs.

Gone, he thought. He knew it was only his imagination, but he was glad to see the lion-headed woman gone all the same.

He bucked up and sat down at the kitchen table, his glass of half-swallowed iced tea next to him. He picked up the scarab pieces and began the process of gluing them together again.

"I'm sorry, Evie," he said to himself. As he worked, he tried to bring back those memories of his wife in the desert, her hair flying wild in the hot wind, her face full of courage and an insatiable sense of adventure. It had been her idea to go into the crypt that day. She had found the scarab covered in dark sand near the tomb, picked it up without hesitation, removed it from that sad resting place.

Such courage.

The guides had named it *ib. Heart.*

They said it was a burial scarab, containing the soul of the deceased, a vessel to take the soul to the afterlife.

Evie smiled. Such a treasure. She clasped the scarab tightly in her hands and took it. Henderson had never loved his wife more than on that hot day in the desert.

He tried to hold onto the image, Evie's fearless eyes defiant against the warnings of the guides. But her face faded; the mirage had shimmered into empty sand.

His hands were steady. The glue sealed between the two pieces; the edges met perfectly. He placed the healed scarab back down on the linoleum and sat back in his chair.

The thunder rumbled again. It seemed as if the ground was shaking from the thunder. Even the door from the kitchen that led out back seemed to shake, as if someone was pounding against it.

The thunder faded. But the pounding against the door continued. Steady. Hard. A heavy hand trying to get in.

Fear seized Bud Henderson's heart. He looked down at the scarab. It was still in one piece, the glue starting to harden.

"Evie!" he cried. "I fixed it! See? All fixed!"

The pounding shook the door frame. The shelves and treasures hanging on the kitchen walls started to rattle. Bud Henderson was sure things would start crashing to the floor, breaking irrevocably.

He picked up the scarab amulet and held it up in front of his face. The glue was drying, the break in the stone healing. But the pounding was getting worse. Scratching sounds accompanied the pounding now, like an animal trying to get in.

"It wasn't me! It was the damned kids!" Henderson was shaking; he could feel his hands getting slippery with sweat as he held the scarab aloft. "Not my fault! The Guerrera boys!" he screamed.

The scratching—heavy, thick claws against the wooden door—had become worse than the pounding. Henderson was sure he heard a vicious snarl on the other side.

He remembered that the guides had begged Evie not to take the scarab. Unholy, they said. The death goddess will find you, they said. Never disturb the *ib*. It contains the soul of one who is dead. A curse follows any who tamper with it.

The night Evie died—her body barely skin and bones, her face as pale as the white sheets of her hospital bed, her lovely hair turned brittle and gray—Bud Henderson clutched the ancient scarab in his hands and dreamed that Evie's soul had taken residence within it. He would always have her with him. The scarab would be her soul.

That's why he kept it in the garden. As his plants grew, so would his memory of Evie. The cucumbers as they blossomed, the beans as they sprouted high: living monuments to his wife's memory.

But the garden never did grow that well. Bud wouldn't admit it, but deep in his heart, he knew it to be true. Sure, the vegetables would swell with water and nutrients—for a time —but then some blight would take them. Year after year. He'd always had a small crop. A small yield. Brown leaves punctured with tiny holes.

Bud didn't believe in curses. It was all nonsense. Evie never put stock in them. Never. She was too strong-willed for that. It was just an old stone.

But the night she had died, Bud dreamed her soul into that stone.

And nothing ever did grow right in the garden afterward.

As he stood trembling in the kitchen, the wild goddess of death clawing at the back door, he held the scarab high in the air. The glue had worked. The amulet was whole again.

"I fixed it, Evie!" he cried into the emptiness of the room. "I did it!"

His hands were so slick with sweat, he could barely hold the scarab steady. His fingers grasped. The scarab slipped.

It hit the kitchen floor and shattered into twenty pieces.

The pounding and scratching on the door stopped. There was silence.

Bud Henderson was numb. Mechanically, he knelt and began to scoop up the broken pieces of the scarab. Their edges were jagged, and one of them cut his finger. Little droplets of red blood sprinkled onto the black stones.

He tried not to think of anyone's soul as he picked up the pieces.

When he went outside, the sun had broken through the grayness of the clouds. It was a muted sunshine, but enough to cause the rainwater on the grass to shimmer. The soil around the cucumbers was soggy, swelled with rain. The trowel dug down deep in the soil.

Bud Henderson scattered the broken scarab pieces like seeds. He covered them with dirt, using his hands to scoop the soil and pat it down. He wiped his hands on his pants, smearing blood and dirt. He stood up, and his bones ached.

Then he went back into the house to have a glass of iced tea and polish the dust from his treasures.

CHAPTER SIX

Shooting Layups at Dusk

IT WAS DUSK, after dinner. Wednesday evening, and Sarah wandered outside to shoot layups. The concrete half-court was a perfect square, the gleaming polycarbonate backboard supported a red metal rim and slightly frayed net. She rolled the red-brown leather ball around on her fingertips. She dribbled. She thought about Avalon.

The half-court had been silent for more than fifteen years. Joe Ray built it for his daughters, but the girls had other plans. Marching band. California. Lives expanded from the squareness of the concrete. But then came the summer of '92, the coming of enchantment, the coming of the wild voices of children, and the clang of rim and leather sounded once more.

Most days, Jay and the Guerrera boys strutted around the court, Rodman and Lambiere and Thomas jerseys flashing in the sun, Sarah languishing on the sidelines.

Except at dusk.

At dusk, it was Sarah's time. The older boys were taken up with flashing screens of MTV and video games so that the allure of pick-up basketball had lost its power.

Alone, Sarah felt the basketball slide across the palms of

her hands. She dribbled as best she could between her legs. She glided toward the hoop and released a layup, a soft touch against the glass, followed by the quiet swooshing of the net. Over and over again, arm outstretched, ball rolling off her fingertips, a dull thud, basket made.

And while she made layups, she told herself stories.

Avalon became an endless country, its woods and glades shimmering into unceasing horizons. Fairies and giants made their castles on high hills and in dark valleys. And the nine queens came slowly, creeping into the seams of rivers and tree bark. First, they bore the elder king away from his bloody battle and healed him beside the nettles of a hawthorn bush. Then they came to rule the country, enchanting it so that dragons and dwarves might roam in the wet leaves and spiders' webs.

Sarah told herself stories and made layups in the pale evening light.

Eventually, the Oak-Hearted Knight made his way to Avalon. He was seeking his lost love, but he was pursued. Hunted. The nine cast him down, enslaved him to sleep, turned him over to the spell of the willow tree. Its great languid vines covered his body like a shawl so that it became hard to tell where the Knight ended and the tree began.

Sarah shot layups, weaved stories under her breath. She dreamed the sunflower hair of the Oak-Hearted Knight, his angular face, his grey-green eyes. She saw the dark outline of his gleaming armor, links of chain mail that coated his body like fish scales. A gauntleted hand grasping a blue-hilted sword. The curl of his lip as he scanned the edge of the darkening forest.

She felt the rustle in the leaves before she heard it. She felt it shiver down her spine. The basketball bounced over the pavement and onto the lawn, a rebound uncaught.

Sarah looked at the edge of the woods and held her breath. A brief outline, a phantom shadow. A man's shape. A sword in silhouette.

The leaves of the trees rustled.

Nothing.

There was no man, no Oak-Hearted Knight. But Sarah's chest pounded, her breath heaving.

Had he been there? On the edge of the woods?

The basketball rested on the grass like a heavy stone. Sarah was alone but the aloneness frightened her. If she moved—she was sure of it—the things hidden in the shadows would get her. If she stepped onto the lawn, she would be that much closer to the woods, that much closer to whatever lurked there, the sinking feeling of eyes that watched and footsteps that moved without a sound. She stood for a long time, an ocean of concrete between her and the ball. And the veil of wooded trees beyond. Something waited within, something lived inside that forest, but Sarah didn't stay to find out.

The screen door clattered. The half-court was empty again. The basketball sat, unclaimed, on Grandpa Ray's front lawn. And the leaves rustled their dusk song to the empty night.

CHAPTER SEVEN

The Watchtower

THE SKY outside the windows was a swirling mixture of rose quartz and amethyst, and floating by like great airships, behemoth clouds puffed and swelled, enormous and staggering in their whiteness. If they weren't so stark white, it would seem like they harbored an approaching thunderstorm.

Around the house, nearer to the grass and dirt and Grandma Ray's flowerbeds, the light was dim, dusky, and grayish as all twilights are in early summer, a haven for rabbits in the endless grass lawns that Grandpa kept trimmed and mowed. It was too soon for fireflies to blink their lamplights, but the bats had begun to circle off in the wide air above the pool and near the edges of the woods.

The woods were dark, shadows upon shadows, the trees fading into the darkness and mixing with the unlit ground. The dead leaves that carpeted the woods were graves for generations of forest dwellers, hallowed ground for squirrels and mice.

"Magic time." Aunt Isabel's face beamed at the children. The last dish was rinsed and stacked next to the sink, the dishrag squeezed and hung to dry, and Isabel wiped her wet hands on her blue jeans.

Sarah squirmed in her chair while she watched her aunt leave the kitchen. Jay sat next to her, trying to stay calm and failing. His leg twitched up and down just like Grandpa Ray's always did. Both children felt like they had a million kernels of corn popping inside them, like the popcorn Grandpa always devoured on the couch when he watched late-night movies.

"They stopped making it in 1982," said Jay, to break the silence. "The computer chip inside was too expensive to manufacture anymore."

"How do you know?" asked Sarah.

"Jaime told me. His dad used to have it. Said it broke and they couldn't find any place to fix it."

"I bet Julian broke it."

Jay shrugged. He wasn't interested in the Guerreras. He wanted to see the thing for himself, to be able to brag the next time he played basketball with Jaime and Julian. His leg twitched faster.

Aunt Isabel returned, a cardboard box in her hands.

Sarah gazed at it: the warlords on horses, the fiery landscape, the ruby-eyed dragon. Swords clashing against spears, storm clouds gathering in the sky. She tried to imagine a dragon in Avalon, and how the queens might enchant it. Would they be masters of the beast, or would it engulf the land in flame? She watched as the box was set down on the kitchen table and felt her body grow as still as a spider on its web.

There, in the center of the garish illustration, towering over the mayhem was the black tower. An obsidian sentinel that loomed like a god of stone and sorcery. The flame-colored lettering across the top of the box named the god: *The Watchtower*. Sarah shivered.

"Cool." Jay reached a hand to remove the lid.

"Better wait." Isabel tousled his hair. "Uncle Jim won't let anyone else touch it."

Sarah's stomach clenched. In all her excitement, she'd forgotten that Uncle Jim would be there. She watched her aunt smile and pour some pop for them to drink. Isabel's face was so young, always smiling, a woman who retained the freedom of youth, like Atalanta chasing the golden apples. Sarah couldn't understand how a man like Jim Zersky had ever managed to woo a woman like that.

"What's it like?" asked Jay.

"Honestly? A bit noisy," Isabel said.

"It's temperamental as hell, that's what it's like." Uncle Jim appeared suddenly, a massive hulk of girth standing in the doorway to the kitchen.

"How was work?" Isabel floated over to him, refusing to acknowledge his grim face, smiling and touching his cheek, and kissing him with warm lips.

Uncle Jim simply shrugged and seemed unaware that his wife overflowed with kindness.

She took his briefcase and set it down on the kitchen table. "We've got Chinese food in the fridge."

"Too late. Ate a burger from the drive-thru."

"Then let's sneak a midnight snack later," Isabel said, squeezing her husband's shoulders and grinning. "I'm laying claim to the Hunan chicken."

Jim grunted and lumbered over to where the children sat. He pulled the box away from their reach. "This isn't a game for kids."

Isabel laughed. "Of course it is! Ages eight and up!"

"It's vintage."

"You're too protective."

"If you don't set it in the grooves properly, it tips right over."

"It's a game."

"And we're out of luck if it breaks. They don't make 'em anymore, you know."

Isabel saw the crestfallen faces of her niece and nephew. Their dreams were trickling down the drain, like the dishwater suds in the sink. "Jim, I promised the kids."

The screen door banged open and shut, and moments later, Grandma Ray came in from watering her tomatoes. She caught sight of her daughter and son-in-law and the kids, all huddled around the box on the table. One look at the black tower was all she needed.

"Wizards and dragons!" she scoffed, shaking her head as if the mere mention of such things was a sufficient insult.

Grandma Ray would never understand something like *The Watchtower*. To her, these fantastical games and make-believe pretending were silly and useless. "Sticking your head in the sand," she would say. It made Sarah so angry that her grandmother didn't understand.

But her grandmother's daughter did. Aunt Isabel wasn't ashamed or afraid of liking the things she liked. And what she liked were wizards and dragons and all the things that Sarah adored. And she read books too. Sometimes Sarah thought she and Aunt Isabel were the only two people in the family who ever read books. Grandma Ray only read clipped articles from *Readers' Digest* and dinner recipes printed in the newspaper.

"Joe, need anything before I sit down?" Grandma called to the living room.

"Bring me a coffee!" answered Grandpa.

Alice Ray mixed the Folger's Instant into a cup with hot water, stirred twice, and retired into the living room with her husband to watch an episode of *Perry Mason*.

Jim glanced at Isabel, the corners of his mouth beginning to smirk. "Well... if it'll annoy your mother..."

Isabel squeezed her husband's shoulder as she sat down at the table. "Thank you, babe."

Jay fist-pumped and shouted "Yes!" while Sarah's stomach leaped. Uncle Jim slowly lifted the lid of the box.

The tiny pieces inside were only cheap molded plastic, and scattered in every corner of the box were dozens of pegboard pins. It was an ordinary board game, an early Eighties artifact of mass-produced junk that had been designed to tap into the sword and sorcery craze of Reagan-era America. But none of that mattered. What mattered was that the game was OLD; it was an unearthed ancient thing that belonged to a time before Sarah could even remember: a hazy, mist-shrouded age that promised adventure, that seemed to live on the edges of the darkest forests, with trails and pathways leading to the dankest of dungeons.

This is what the early Eighties promised. It was an uncharted time when fantasy sprang from the well at the world's end and burst upon suburban streets. When Uncle Jim lifted the box lid, Sarah could smell trolls and tombs buried with barbarian treasures, and the soggy wet earth where fairy rings sprouted, and the hot, terrible, gold-tinged breath of a dragon.

"This..." said Uncle Jim, lifting the heavy black obelisk from the box, "...is it." He held it aloft like an idol. As Isabel spread the game board on the table, Jim fitted the tower into the shallow indentations at the center of the cardboard. The

Watchtower stood precariously atop the surface; Sarah worried that any bump or shake of the kitchen table might topple the mighty statue. But even still, it was an ominous, grim sight: the Watchtower was the master of this world, a hideous presence that revealed nothing and threatened everything. Its dark opacity portended doom and promised a gallery of horrors within.

Sarah's imagination could hardly contain all that was conjured within the black walls of the Watchtower: foul goblins with yellowed teeth, a wicked sorcerer whose skin was cursed with dragon scales, a venomous basilisk. A coven of witches; a den of crooked queens. All of it and more could be hidden behind the Watchtower's walls. Though made of plastic and marred by a small rectangular computer screen at its base, the tower still commanded an obscene power. It still reeked of dank dungeons and foul treasures. It still radiated the magic of an older time, a more dangerous time. In its stillness and silence, the Watchtower was more fearsome than any slavering monster. Its formless, faceless, inscrutable facade meant that all of Sarah's nightmares and dreams could be contained within.

Sarah grinned. This was more than she had hoped for. Though the flimsy plastic game pieces and blandly painted board were uninspired, and the pegboards and tally sheets made for a dull game, the tower itself was a thing alien to this world: a talisman that could bewitch them all. And Sarah was ready to be bewitched.

Smirking, Uncle Jim pressed the black button beneath the tower's tiny computer screen. The Watchtower jangled to life. 8-bit music blared out of the small speaker, a tinny flourish of trumpets heralding the beginning of a computerized quest.

Words materialized on the gray screen: *Defeat the dragon and destroy its lair... Destroy the Watchtower!*

The words exploded into a thousand firecracker pixels, and Sarah realized she was holding her breath, and Jay rocked back and forth in his chair; Uncle Jim folded his arms across his chest—looking ready to thump it like a gorilla—and his heavy-lidded eyes glared with satisfaction at the plastic tower and the sway it held upon the children, while Isabel smiled placidly, seemingly unaware of the magic she was witnessing.

For a moment, Sarah unlocked her gaze from the tower and caught sight of her aunt: Isabel's eyes wandered toward the open window behind Uncle Jim's head, toward the darkening forest outside, and the fireflies, who now emerged from their hidden resting places and danced upon the twilight air, and Sarah's eyes wandered too, toward the shifting shadows of dusk, toward the summer night, toward the valley and the wooded hills beyond, toward the old barn which stood haunted in the vacant field, toward the headstone which marked the fox's grave, toward the kingdom of the nine queens.

Toward the rusted gates.

Sarah shivered as she thought of those wrought iron gates blanketed with gloaming darkness, and the key she kept hidden in an empty shoebox. A dark shadow loomed behind those rusted gates: a high tower, formless and faceless and shrouded in danger.

"Does the youngest go first?" Isabel's question was warmed by her smile, a generous offering. But Sarah wasn't listening. She was in her mind, racing through the garden with the fireflies, trying to catch the magic that would save Avalon.

"Not if she's lost in her head and not listening to the rules," said Jim. "Sarah!"

He brought his arm up quickly and snapped his fingers in her face. But the sudden movement, the jerking arm, the bullying peevishness were too much: Jim's body rocked the table, and the tower shook, and the grooves proved too shallow and ill-made, and with a heavy thud, the Watchtower tumbled.

It flopped over like a dead fish. When Jim realized what he had done, he swung his arm back without thinking, trying to catch something that had already fallen. It was that furious swing that pushed the game board across the table and sent the tower rolling to its doom.

They all stood over it. Red and blue electric wires were visible through the cracked plastic, like veins exposed. The silence was harsher than any din; it was a spearpoint through the gut. Sarah could feel her uncle's face reddening, the room growing hot with dragon breath, and the black incantations swelling upon Jim Zersky's lips. She didn't want to look, she didn't want to hear, she didn't want to be anywhere near that broken, ugly thing that sat on the linoleum floor like some cracked skull.

But it was just a toy. Just a piece in a game. Sarah tried to convince herself, and she held the lump in her throat hoping it would dissolve and she could breathe again. When Uncle Jim's words came spilling out of his mouth, they were like spiked boulders and casks of hot oil catapulted over castle walls; they were a battering ram thrust at the child's heart, and Sarah's ears burned, and her cheeks popped with crimson blood.

All her fault, she made him do it, not paying attention, irreplaceable, ruined, ruined, ruined, and the evidence was right there, on the floor, the Watchtower destroyed.

But the dragon was not defeated. It raged and made wrath

and rained down fire. Not even tears could put out such fury. Its eyes burned red.

Until at last, Isabel's voice broke into the flames and quelled them. Everything was over, and she would clean up the mess. Why didn't the kids go watch TV with Grandma and Grandpa? Why didn't they run outside and play one last game in the dusk? Up to their room, or down to the basement, or anywhere else, but not here, not in the wreckage, not in the wasteland.

Sarah didn't want to go outside. Somehow, when she looked, all the fireflies were gone.

"You were the one who knocked it over, Jim."

Sarah didn't want to hear, but she lingered just at the foot of the steps to her room.

"Just pick it up. If you hadn't promised them—"

"But I did," Isabel said.

"You owe me a new game."

"You sound like a baby."

"Just pick it up."

"Do you want me to save the pieces?"

Sarah heard the shuffle of a chair being pushed, and footsteps, and then the clang of the screen door. After a long moment of silence, something heavy and shattered was dumped into the garbage can. And when she could feel footsteps coming around the corner, she fled, up the stairs and into the darkness.

THEY SAT on the child's bed. Sarah wiped away her tears, but the wetness still clung to her cheeks. Isabel put an arm around her. They sat in silence for a long time, hanging upon a thread of filament, waiting for someone to cut the string and release their fear. Isabel knew she should be the one to start, to offer something of comfort or apology. She was the adult, after all. But it was Sarah who spoke first.

"Uncle Jim is mean."

Isabel flinched. With all the bluntness of a heavy brick, the child had laid bare a truth Isabel didn't want to admit.

"Not all the time," Isabel said, her voice tottering on shoddy grooves.

"Most of the time."

"He's… He just has a hard time with kids."

"Because he's mean. Mean people don't like kids. He didn't have to get so mad about the game."

"It wasn't your fault." The words came out of Isabel by instinct. She had thought them so many times before, in other arguments, in other times when Jim's anger had swelled.

"Why do want to be with someone so mean?"

Isabel looked away. Her eyes were dry and wet at the same time, and the dryness made the tears well up, and the wetness made them spill over the edges.

"It's not that simple, Sarah."

"But he's not nice. And you are."

"Uncle Jim was mean tonight. And he shouldn't have been. But he's not like that always. He's a lot more than his meanness."

Sarah didn't see why that mattered. Wasn't his meanness enough? Her mom had never said it, but Sarah knew her dad had been mean too, the kind of mean that others couldn't see. It had been enough to make Mom leave.

"It wasn't your fault," Isabel repeated.

Sarah clenched her teeth. "It was just a cheap piece of plastic."

Isabel laughed, a little hiccup of a thing, but it broke the dike in her eyes, and tears flowed down her cheeks. "Very cheap."

Sarah moved closer; she wanted to put their warmth together. "He was being stupid."

"He was," Isabel answered. "But I promised to love him even when he's being stupid."

Sarah put her arms around Isabel's stomach and squeezed. "Well," Sarah replied, "I didn't."

Isabel laughed again and kissed her niece on the head, letting her lips rest on the child's soft hair. "I wish it weren't so complicated."

"I don't think it's complicated," Sarah said. "We shouldn't let the monsters win. The bullies and the bad guys."

Isabel hugged her niece tighter. "It's good to fight for what's right. I'm proud of you for wanting that."

Sarah smiled.

"But people are complicated," Isabel continued. "Even when we think we know a person, we don't always know everything. Each of us is a little good and a little bad, even if we don't want to admit it."

Sarah had her doubts. She remembered Uncle Jim's eyes and his red, furious face. "Uncle Jim should try being a little more good."

Isabel's heart felt like it was sitting in the center of the game board, beating bloody red in the fluorescent kitchen lights. She squeezed back more of those dry, wet tears. "Yeah." She held Sarah tighter. "Definitely."

They sat in silence for a long time. Isabel found a way to swallow the lingering tears, and Sarah's body felt calm against her chest.

"Come on." Isabel stood up, and at first, she thought Sarah

was going to shake her head. The child's face was still downcast, and her shoulders were slumped. "Come with me. I have another box to show you."

This was a good mystery. Sarah's curiosity took hold and she felt the muscles in her body flex with life again. Isabel smiled impishly and led her niece from the children's bedroom to the hallway that connected to Alice and Joe's room.

The Rays' upstairs hallway was not quite a hallway at all; it was more of a landing, with a bathroom on one side, the Rays' bedroom on the other, and then the winding staircase going down on the far side. But next to the staircase, nuzzled in the corner and narrowed by a slanting ceiling, was a small white door—perfectly square—framed by white moldings. It was shorter in height than Sarah and had only a little white knob for a handle. Sarah had noticed it before, many times, and always wondered what was inside. She assumed it was some sort of closet, and that its small doorway was due to the steepness of the slanted ceiling.

"Here," said Isabel, "is some old magic from before the dawn of *The Watchtower*, or any cheap plastic board game." She knelt and grabbed the handle of the little door. At first, it wouldn't open, so Isabel shoved it with her shoulder, and then there was the snap of swollen wood breaking away from humid paint, and the door creaked open.

Sarah peered in, mesmerized by this tiny hidden room at the top of the stairs. It was cramped, but Sarah could see that the room extended far back into the bowels of the house. She was afraid to go too far in, to get lost in the darkness. But Isabel was made of sterner stuff and dove right into the cobwebbed boxes and bric-a-brac that crowded the space.

"What is this place?" Sarah managed to ask, daring to peek her head in to see what her aunt was doing.

"It's just part of the attic."

Sarah was too afraid to look into the back. It was so narrow and dark. It reminded Sarah too much of her nightmares, where she would descend into a darkened basement that seemed to have no end. The fear of not knowing, of not being able to see what was within the swelling shadows was too much for her to bear. She waited outside, in the light of the open landing.

Aunt Isabel grunted and slid something heavy out of the cramped space.

"This," said Isabel, "is a box worth opening. At least, I hope so."

A heavy brown cardboard box lay at their feet, cobwebs billowing off it like streamers. Isabel knelt and pulled open the box's lids, and immediately Sarah could see the jeweled covers of paperbacks. Their corners were worn and the pages were yellowed, but they were still a trove of unearthed treasures. The hoard of ancient lore had been recovered, the gems of the dungeon discovered.

"Go ahead, Sarah. Do more than stare. Here—" Isabel took one from the box and handed it to her niece "—this was my favorite."

Inked lines unraveled across the front and back covers like spider webs, catching within them an image of a young girl looking out from a parapet, with a small jade-green dragon woven around her arm. The girl stared out at something unseen, something heavy and sad and difficult, something that meant she would have to grow up soon and face an uncertain, unwelcome world.

Sarah knew that look; she wondered if this paperback was

simply a mirror, and for a moment she had been able to catch a glimpse of her own reflection. Her aunt was watching her, that sad smile in her eyes, and Sarah knew Aunt Isabel had once seen a reflection in that book cover too.

"I'll help you carry the box back to your room," Isabel said after a long silence.

Sarah realized she'd forgotten to say thank you. "Aunt Isabel…"

"Don't worry," replied her aunt. "I should be thanking you. You don't know how long I've kept these books up here, waiting, wondering what to do with them."

"I'll take good care of them."

"I know you will."

CHAPTER EIGHT

The Card Game

"WHERE IS YOUR MOTHER, DEAR?" Mrs. Fabrizio smiled, eyes twinkling with warmth. Her round face always seemed to be smiling.

The perfect grandmother, Sarah thought. Her own grandma laughed and smiled easily enough, but not so much when she talked to Sarah. Mrs. Fabrizio was different; she seemed to be made of warmth and kindness, all kinds of joy squished into her squat and stout body.

The old woman's question wasn't accusatory, Sarah knew that, but still, it made her stomach lurch. "California," Sarah answered. "She said it was a two-month shoot."

"That'll keep her busy, I suppose. Hard to mind a couple of kids with that kind of schedule." Mrs. Fabrizio sighed. "I remember when Annie was a young thing just about your age. Always playing dress-up and acting out her funny little plays. You're a dreamer too. Probably why Alice is so hard on you." Lina Fabrizio winked at Sarah just as Grandma Ray came back in from watering her plants.

"Did you shuffle the cards?" Alice Ray asked.

Every Thursday afternoon, Lina Fabrizio came over, had a

cup of coffee with cream, dipped her biscotti into the cup, and played cards with Grandma Ray.

"I did." Mrs. Fabrizio set the deck on the table, and Alice Ray cut the deck.

The game was gin rummy, something Sarah had watched every week since summer began, but the rules and strategy escaped her. She didn't come to watch the card game, though; she came to hear the stories.

"Go into my purse, honey," Mrs. Fabrizio said with a wink. "A little treat."

Sarah expected to find a caramel or hard strawberry candy, the usual old lady treats. Her eyes widened, though, and her fingers began to tremble when she laid hands on the surprise in Mrs. Fabrizio's purse.

"Not what you were expecting, eh?" said Lina, eyes twinkling.

Sarah held the gift in her hands and stared open-mouthed.

"What's so special?" Alice Ray asked, eyes narrowed. To her mind, it looked like Sarah was holding a couple of old coins.

"Remember Theo spent all that time in France after the liberation? He found these in an old wooden chest in a farmhouse in Alsace. For heaven's sake, Alice, we talked about it two weeks ago!"

"Are they really real?" Sarah asked, still dazed by the gift.

"Never had 'em checked, but I should think so," answered Lina. "Look old enough to be."

"But what the hell are they?" Alice couldn't see the use of two old, half-crumbled coins.

"They're medieval. Reign of Charlemagne." Sarah said it to herself more than to her grandmother.

Lina Fabrizio beamed and gently banged the kitchen table in triumph. "Knew you'd like 'em!"

"Let's get on with the game," said Alice. "Your deal, Lina."

Sarah barely watched the first hand. She held the two Carolingian coins with reverence, then she started examining them more carefully, letting her fingers run over the inscriptions and the images embossed in the silver. *Two real medieval coins. Over one thousand years old.* Sarah's imagination began to overload with stories, ideas, and unbidden thoughts of Avalon.

Something to bargain with the queens of Avalon? she wondered to herself. Did the queens of Avalon need to be bargained with? Sarah decided they did. And she decided that it was only by offering payment that the queens would let the Oak-Hearted Knight go.

"What should we talk about this time?" Mrs. Fabrizio asked. "I haven't told you about the shipwreck near Guam, have I? Ernie came to me in a dream when it happened."

"I thought he came to your mother in a dream," interjected Alice.

Lina waved her hand as if waving away a fly. "We both had the dream. And my papa said he felt salt water in his mouth instead of saliva in the very moment when Ernie's boat capsized."

Sarah came out of her daydream long enough to realize what the two women were talking about. "Who's Ernie?"

"My brother," said Lina. "Served with Joe for a while, but then got switched off the aircraft carrier to a smaller transport, and ended up shipwrecked."

"During the war?"

Lina nodded and played a card from her hand.

"Was it a bomber? Did a kamikaze pilot sink the ship?" Sarah's imagination raced.

Lina chuckled. "Nothing that dramatic. Just a typhoon."

A typhoon was plenty dramatic for Sarah. She imagined the horrible wave that took down the transport, spilling water through all the decks, drowning men, tearing apart the steel of the hull.

"How did he survive?" she asked, wide-eyed again. Sarah's eyes were often wide with wonder when Mrs. Fabrizio told one of her stories.

"He said my mother's name. And my name too. And we heard him in our dreams, and Mama called out to him and sent a prayer to his guardian angel. And when Papa tasted the salt water in his mouth, he sat up straight in his bed and said, 'Something's happened to Ernie,' and we all got up and started a novena, right there, in the middle of the night, while Ernie was half a world away, shipwrecked in the ocean. And when the night was nearly over, Mama said she knew Ernie was safe, that he'd washed ashore."

Alice played a card, then Lina. Sarah realized she'd been holding her breath.

"We got a telegram a few months later, found out he'd washed up on Guam and somehow fell in with another company. He got shipped to a California hospital not long after that."

"Did you really have a dream about your brother, Mrs. Fabrizio?" Sarah asked. She wanted to believe, but the look on her grandmother's face was stoic and skeptical.

"Honest to God's truth. We told Ernie when he came back that we had the dreams, and what time it was when Papa tasted the salt water, and Ernie said that was the exact time the wave hit."

"I'm just glad Joe stayed on the aircraft carrier," said Alice. "I'm out." She laid down her final cards, discarded one, and took the victory.

"Well, damn," said Lina, wrinkling her nose but still smiling at the corners of her mouth. "Get me another cup of coffee, Sarah, will you? Heavy on the cream." She unwrapped another cellophane-coated biscotti and dabbed at the crumbs on the table with her forefinger. "I'll play another hand, Alice, if you want."

When Sarah had brought the elderly woman her coffee, she sat down next to Lina and looked at the medieval coins again.

"What'll you do with them?" Mrs. Fabrizio asked. "Gonna write a story?"

Sarah was embarrassed to nod, even though the old woman had guessed the truth.

"Just like Annie, with your stories."

Alice Ray dealt the cards in a flash. She seemed determined to win the next round.

"What's Annie working on this time?" Lina asked, coffee and biscotti mixing with her words.

Sarah squirmed in her seat, stomach lurching again. She knew the question was directed at her grandmother, but she still felt interrogated.

"Oh, one of those 'very important films' she's always going on about. So important they never seem to end up getting finished."

"And the money?"

"What you'd expect."

"And Scottie?"

Alice didn't answer right away. Sarah felt her

grandmother's eyes shift toward her, a look of concern, maybe, or perhaps fear.

"London, I guess. That's what Annie said last time she mentioned him."

Sarah made sure not to hear. She held the coins tightly and disappeared into Avalon.

CHAPTER NINE

The Book Depot

THE BOOKSELLER LOOKED like an overgrown dwarf. Stout and bearded, he sat on a stool behind the checkout counter, most likely, Sarah thought, because otherwise, he'd have trouble seeing over it. What little hair he had on his head was white, but most of his scalp was covered with shiny pink skin, and his cheeks were that pale pinkish hue of someone who didn't get much sunlight. His beard was long and white. *Like Santa Claus*, thought Sarah. And he wore wire-rimmed spectacles like Santa too, right on the end of his bulbous nose.

But the bookseller was not jolly. Not in the least. His beady eyes scanned the store for any hint of a child's sneakers gamboling about the store, or a smiling face peering behind the comic book racks. He listened like a hawk, perched on his stool, wary of any sound of childlike laughter.

He had to be wary, of course, because children weren't interested in books. No siree, they were not! They were interested in the candy stacked on the candy display, and the magazines splayed out on the magazine shelves. They were interested in sneaking and stealing and using the bookseller's shortened stature and stout limbs to their advantage. If he was shelving books amongst the stacks, he was too short to see the entrance, and if he was behind his counter helping a customer, the wall of the candy display blocked his limited view. And if he did hear children giggling and no doubt sneaking a pack of Swizzle Stix or a Fun Dip, if he was off in the back of the store, his short legs made him waddle instead of run to catch them, and most times, his waddle was not enough. There had been ten candy thefts since school had let out in early June. Not to mention the pilfered magazines.

When Sarah came in and the bell above the door jangled, she heard the bookseller clear his throat, threatening a gruff, wordless warning. He was behind the counter, hidden from view by the wall of the candy display, but listening nevertheless: a wary hawk on his three-legged crag.

Sarah wasn't interested in candy or magazines. She was a bemusing creature for the bookseller because she was a child who actually wanted books. He distrusted her, but he also couldn't deny that she was sometimes a paying customer. Most days, though, she was a browser, and such behavior raised his suspicion. Scanning the spines of the Science Fiction and Fantasy section, she would trace her finger along the gem-colored covers. She didn't fool the bookseller. She was a child like all the others, and no child was really interested in reading. Not when they had beeping and booping arcade games, television screens, and Walkman radios.

But this child, this skinny, brown-haired mouse with bright red sneakers brushed right past the candy, paid not a single glance at the magazines. She didn't even go down her familiar haunt, the Science Fiction and Fantasy section. She came right up to the counter, determined and somewhat out of breath. Then she spoke to the bookseller, even tried looking him in the eye.

"Are there any books about... magic gates? Or... sorcerer queens? Or knights trapped in a deep sleep, on a quest, that sort of thing?" The child's hands were squeezed tight into nervous fists. She spoke too quickly, and she looked away once the bookseller peered down at her over his glasses. "I want something maybe with a unicorn on the cover." Her last request was feeble, weak-voiced. She knew it sounded ridiculous even as she said it, but the words couldn't be put back into her mouth.

The bookseller said nothing. He grunted a little. Perhaps it was a suppressed belch. But he certainly didn't answer. He drummed his fingers on the countertop, staring all the time at Sarah, trying to suss out what she meant. And whether she was really interested in such a book or merely bothering him. Most likely she was bothering him. Couldn't she see he was tallying up receipts? That he was busy? That he didn't have time for inane questions?

He slid off his stool with a heavy sigh. On the ground, his chin barely reached over the counter, but his stumpy legs carried him swiftly to the other side, to the merchandise floor, to the stacks and stacks of books that were too tightly shelved within the too-small store. Sarah followed him as he waddled to the back corner, to the section nearest the door marked "Do Not Enter" and the storeroom behind it.

"Here," he said, "these are all speculative fiction. Have a look for yourself." He waved a dismissive hand at the bookshelf and then pushed past her to resume his perch behind the counter.

Sarah's stomach sank. This was the same old Science Fiction and Fantasy section she always browsed. She'd been up and down the stacks so many times she had memorized every title. She tried to look over the shelves to find the bookseller again, to catch his eye. But a customer was at the counter, blocking her view, and she could hear the jangle of the cash register as the patron completed his purchase.

Sarah waited. The gray-haired customer thanked the bookseller with a quick word and a wave, then turned to leave. Sarah watched the old curmudgeon slump onto his stool and rest his hands on his potbelly. Receipts sat in a disheveled stack nearby, while the plastic calculator and pencil waited patiently for their work to resume. But the bookseller's fingers didn't move from their resting place. And his eyes, though closed, were not eager to look upon their former work. Instead, with another heavy sigh, the man slid down from his perch and walked back toward Sarah. She looked away, pretending to browse the books, but she listened and watched out of the corner of her eye.

He was just testing her, she thought. Just making sure she was a real reader, had a true heart. But when the bookseller walked down the stacks on the other side, out of sight, and then abruptly through the storeroom door, Sarah's true heart sank, and the "Do Not Enter" sign mocked her. She wondered for a moment if maybe she might just get a different book, one of the dozens she had browsed since summer began. She had money after all. All those chores for Grandpa Ray, her Christmas money saved up too; she could probably buy two books and still have some change left over. The DragonSpear series looked intriguing; they seemed to promise stories of high adventure and a lot of bloodshed. The dragons were fierce, and the knights and wizards were dark-eyed and savage. Or maybe one of the Yaxinth books with their weird creatures, colorful covers, and off-beat titles: *A Spell for Salamander*; *Golem, Golem*; *Harpy on a Pedestal*.

But as Sarah plucked a few books from the shelf and read their back covers, she knew that none of them was what she wanted. None of them cracked open her imagination, none of them thrilled her heart and made her long for another world. If only there was something like her tales of Avalon, of the nine queens, of the Knight and his quest... Of the Rusted Gates. They were the world Sarah really wanted, the world she really longed to escape into.

The storeroom door swung open suddenly and the bookseller emerged, red-faced, puffing a bit from exertion, and holding a slim paperback book. He didn't careen around to the other aisle this time; he headed straight for Sarah. He thrust the book at her.

"This is what you want," he said, staring at her unblinkingly.

She hesitated, and the man practically shoved the book into her hands. Sarah took it and looked down at the cover. She knew the bookseller was still watching her, and she felt her face grow red. The cover of the slim volume was mostly a swirl of greens and blues: blues for sky and soft grey clouds, and greens for the leafy trees and tall grass. And in the center of what appeared to be a glade was a glorious grey-white unicorn, rearing up on its hind legs, mane of pale golden hair waving in the unseen breeze. Then, to Sarah's amazement and sudden fear, she saw what was illustrated behind the unicorn: a pair of wrought iron gates, cold and hard, dark as shadows. They guarded no one and enclosed nothing.

The book almost fell from her hands. Her fingers trembled so much, and her body shook too, that she didn't dare to speak or move for fear that she would drop the book or buckle at the knees.

"It's the greatest fantasy novel you will ever read," said the bookseller in a flat, superior sort of voice. "If you have the guts."

Then he walked past her, sweating and waddling hurriedly as if ten customers were queued up at the cash register. But the store was empty except for Sarah, and she didn't move.

Gates to Illvelion.

It was a thin book. Barely 200 pages.

A. R. Rathmann.

The name meant nothing to her, but the mysterious initials conjured an image of A. R. Rathmann in Sarah's imagination: a dark-browed wizard in a fez, haunting the hallways of his vast mansion, surrounded by living statues and a talking griffon, by gargoyles and crystal decanters filled with bizarre concoctions.

The edges of the book looked worn and creased; many years and many fingers had taken their toll. The paper was yellowed, but in all other ways, the book was in good condition. The spine was strong, and when Sarah fanned through the pages, she felt a good snap and slight stiffness to the paper that made her smile. This was a book that could withstand a reader. It wasn't one of those old used books that wilted at the touch and started to lose pages like petals on a delicate rose. As she flipped through it, chapter titles caught her eye.

"The Glass Pool of the Hidden West." "Gallien, the Unicorn." "The Iron Key."

Sarah stopped. That tingly, creepy feeling from before came back to make her shiver. The gates, an iron key, a world that seemed to mirror her own.

Her hand almost set the book down on top of the nearby bookshelf. The safeness of the DragonSpear books beckoned, with their unremarkable knights and wizards. The comfortable weirdness of the Yaxinth series gave her an escape, a chance to turn away from this book the bookseller had given her. There were other books too: familiar books, books she'd browsed a dozen times, books that would have adventure, and magic, and all the other things she enjoyed.

But *Gates to Illvelion* didn't leave her hands. Her fingers couldn't let go even as they trembled. When she laid it down on the checkout counter, the bookseller said nothing. He rang it up, took her money, and handed her the change. But as he slipped a bookmark in between the pages and handed her the book, Sarah thought she caught a glint in his eyes and a slight smile upon his lips.

The bell above the door rang loudly as the child left, the heat from the summer sun billowing into the coolness of the store for a brief moment. The bookseller rested his fat fingers on top of his belly and closed his eyes. He pictured something in his mind's eye—an old dream, perhaps, or the memories of a story with a unicorn and sorcerer queens and a knight trapped in a deep sleep—but what he saw, only he could tell, and he said nothing.

Sarah stopped outside the store, the blazing sun streaming onto the sidewalk despite the canopied roof over the shopping center. She opened the book and pulled out the bookmark. Emblazoned on a sky-blue background was a white unicorn reared up on its hind legs. Underneath were the words, "A Book Is a Journey You Can Travel Again and Again." Carefully, Sarah put the bookmark back into the pages, marking the beginning of chapter one. Then she rode her bike home to begin her quest.

CHAPTER TEN

Balsam Wood

"Today, Grandpa?"

Not today. Joe Ray had to go to the hardware store and pick up some ten-inch screws. And no, Sarah couldn't come with him to the hardware store. He didn't need a kid underfoot to mess around. He needed his ten-inch screws and that was that.

Sarah wasn't interested in hardware, not really, but she thought if maybe she could go and look around, and see what was on the shelves, she might find something to help Grandpa Ray make her sword. A special kind of wood, maybe. Or paint for the hilt. Or a saw that might cut the edges just right.

Sarah knew nothing about woodworking or tools or anything like that, but she knew how she wanted her sword. Strong, unbreakable, a champion's sword.

Instead, Grandpa promised her he'd make it out of balsam wood and help her hammer in the nails herself, so she could take some ownership and have some pride in her own work.

Sarah knew Grandpa meant well. She knew he was trying to teach her something, something important about life and work and being grown up. And she did want to go inside his workshop, try out his tools, smell the burnt grease and tang of iron wrenches. To be allowed in his sanctuary was a special privilege.

She hadn't much idea what balsam wood was or whether she could swing a hammer or wield a saw, but she wanted her sword. It felt silly to say it out loud or even to think the thought too directly, but Sarah knew that the sword would help her find Avalon. She knew it as clearly as she knew the old skeleton key would open the gates.

Grandpa left for the hardware store, and Sarah spent the morning reading. She read haphazardly, picking up books out of the box Aunt Isabel had given her, reading their back covers, flipping through the first couple of chapters, wanting to be captivated, but always coming away unmoved, always tossing the book back into the box and grabbing another.

The new book from the Book Depot—the one with the rusted gates—sat next to her pillow, wedged between the cotton sheets and the wall. She hadn't dared read it. Not yet. The time wasn't right.

That's what she told herself.

Instead, she pawed through the old books in the cardboard box and grazed among the pages. All the while, she was really thinking of Avalon, and how badly she needed a sword.

Joe Ray came back around 11:30 and Grandma made him lunch. After that, he said, he needed to mow the lawn. Maybe tomorrow, he said. Find him early, he said, and they could start sawing the wood, maybe finish before ten o'clock. Gotta be early, though. Otherwise, the day will go to waste.

Early for Grandpa Ray was 5:30 a.m. Sarah had never gotten up before 7:30 in her life, and the only time she managed to get up that early was a couple of years back when the CBS Saturday morning cartoon schedule put her favorite show on earlier. She realized after a few weeks of forcing herself out of bed that maybe she was getting too old for cartoons about little blue people in white hats.

But Grandpa was an early bird. Better for catching worms, he said. You'll sleep when you're dead, he said. But Sarah liked sleeping too much to get up at 5:30 in the morning.

She liked the death of sleep and the peace of dreams, and even the desire for a sword couldn't rouse her. Not in summer. Not when she could sleep in whenever she wanted and wait for the sun to wake her, and savor the smell of Grandma's eggs frying and sausage sizzling, and let her dreams linger for just a minute or two, or maybe twenty, and exist somewhere between the edges of the tangled forest and the cool dew drops of Faerie and her soft bedsheets.

Then one afternoon, while Sarah was watching old reruns and hadn't gone outside all day, Grandpa Ray came out of the kitchen and said, "Coming to make that sword of yours?"

Sarah materialized in the garage in an instant.

Just scraps. Leftover pieces from the lumber yard. Flattened sticks about as long as Sarah's arm. Nothing like swords. Sarah held one in her hands and felt its lightness. She could snap it in half if she tried. *How could these ever fight ogres or dragons?*

Grandpa held up two of the pieces and put one on top of the other, perpendicular. "We'll cut one down smaller, then hammer it together here, see?"

But all Sarah could see was a flimsy wooden cross, like the kind stuck in the dirt atop a grave.

"Get me the hand-saw," said Joe Ray. "I'll show you how to clamp it so it doesn't move when you cut."

Somewhere in the northeast of America, deep in a Maine forest or the Minnesota wilderness, was the balsam fir tree that produced these few sticks. Somewhere in a Midwestern home at Christmas, a balsam fir sat in a living room, strung with lights and colored bulbs, with presents resting beneath it like ripe fruit. And somewhere in the mists of bygone days, a Potawatomi woman along the shores of Lake Superior chewed the balsam fir needles to heal her illness and her pain.

But for Sarah Lewis, on a summer afternoon in Michigan in the last decade of the twentieth century, the thin piece of balsam she clamped to the vice grip was no Christmas tree or healing plant. It was a crude, sad, flimsy stick that looked about as much like a sword as a pencil or a wooden ruler.

She felt foolish, thinking about the sword she had imagined. Somehow in her head, she'd come up with the idea that Grandpa would help her make a real sword: made of wood, sure, but carved and crafted to look true, with a blade that tapered to a dull point, and a sturdy cross-guard, a smooth grip she could wrap with strips of leather, maybe, and a rounded pommel at the end, something she could imagine was made of silver or gold. Looking at the two pieces of balsam wood her grandfather had found for her, she realized how silly her dream had been.

It wasn't that Joe Ray didn't have the skill. He had built all kinds of things from scratch: a picnic table, the swing set on the front lawn, the deck around the pool. Sarah knew that Grandpa could fix just about anything that needed fixing around the house. It wasn't a matter of skill. Sarah was sure that if her grandfather had wanted to, he'd have designed and built a sword to rival Excalibur.

But Grandpa didn't think about that. He hadn't the faintest notion that Sarah could want something that would look so real, and be so real. He knew she played funny games out in the woods with the neighbor boy, that she got lost in her books the way his daughter Isabel once did, that she liked to tell stories to herself when she thought nobody was listening.

Joe Ray knew his granddaughter had a big imagination, and he loved her for it.

But it was not his imagination.

When Sarah had asked him to help her build a sword, he thought of something that she could do herself, something he could teach her how to do. A simple project: a few ends to saw off, a few nails to hammer in, some sandpaper for the rough edges. He liked the idea of helping his granddaughter learn to use some tools. Something useful. A good project for a kid.

Sarah's eyes drifted away from the work table.

"Alright, grab the hammer." Joe Ray showed her how to hold the nail and how to hit it with the hammer so her fingers wouldn't get caught, and he watched her give it a try, but she barely tapped the nail, seemed reluctant, or maybe not interested. "Here, I'll show you again."

She was afraid of the hammer. Afraid to make a mistake and catch her fingers. Joe held the nail and told her to hit it, slowly, with small taps, until the metal made its indent in the wood.

But her small taps were feather-dust, her hands weak as they fumbled with the hammer. Joe did it himself while Sarah watched, first one nail, then another. Just two was all it needed.

When they were done, Joe Ray hoped his granddaughter would feel the satisfaction of building something with her own two hands.

But when he looked at the sword—just two pieces of flimsy balsam—the scales fell suddenly from his eyes.

This wasn't what she wanted. This wasn't like the stories she'd tell herself up in her room or out shooting layups after dinner. This was just two pieces of wood hammered together with two tiny nails. He knew it now.

"There you go," he said. His voice was flat even as he tried to smile. "Learned a new skill."

It wasn't what he wanted to say. He'd tried to put his words into the hammering and the sawing and the quick movements of the sandpaper. Into showing his granddaughter how to do something.

"Thank you, Grandpa."

She took the sword and ran off. Down the driveway, off to the woods. If she hated it, she didn't show it.

The grass on the sloping lawn behind the house was getting longer by the second. Joe Ray didn't waste another breath standing alone in the garage; the mower beckoned, the work still to be done.

Let the child imagine, he thought while he turned the key and started the machine.

CHAPTER ELEVEN

Cicadas on the Pavement

"Can your grandpa make one for me?"

"Really?" Sarah was embarrassed just to be holding the balsam wood sword. It looked so crude, barely even a toy, just two skinny planks of wood notched together.

"Yeah! We can have sword fights, more adventures like the kind where we fought the hedge snake by the creek, or those trolls at the bottom of the hill, that kinda stuff." Alex held out his hand. "Can I hold it?"

Sarah let him have it, and Alex beamed, swinging it and stabbing imaginary goblins.

"Yeah," he said, looking it over, turning it in his hands. "Yeah, I'd like one too."

The sword felt heavier when Sarah received it back. She gripped the hilt tighter. "I can make it for you."

"You can?"

"Yeah, Grandpa showed me how. All the steps. I used the saw and the clamp thing. Hammered in the nails." Sarah caught herself. "Actually, Grandpa did that part. But I know how!" she added quickly. "It's not hard. We just gotta get the stuff."

"Let's go!"

They were off, running with summer feet, barefoot and hot on the asphalt and dry grass, nothing to stop them. The forge and the hammer awaited their arrival.

But after trying to find two good pieces of balsam, and struggling to loosen the clamp, and a splinter in Sarah's left index finger, they gave up. They swept the sawdust away and went to lay in the grass. They stared up at the clouds and the late afternoon sky while the buzz of cicadas hummed all around them.

"What is that sound?" Sarah asked.

Alex didn't know. A bird or a bug, he figured. Maybe an airplane or radio tower or something. Neither knew anything about cicadas.

"It's strange," replied Sarah.

"Yeah."

The one thing about summer that Sarah hated was the bugs. The insects all around her grandparents' house were strange. Tiny, hideous monsters, worse than the imaginary hedge snake she had conjured out of her head while playing with Alex, or the cockroaches she would find in the apartment back in California.

But in the lawns and woods and driveways of her grandparents' property, the bugs came in all sorts of shapes and colors and terrible forms. Daddy longlegs would sprawl up and down the white stucco walls of the house's exterior; praying mantises would creep over leaves and along branches; emerald-backed beetles and mutated dragonflies and vicious black-bodied alien wasps would invade the shed, or the pool deck, or the garage. And at night, the mosquitoes would feast.

The only joy was watching the bumblebees in Grandma's flower garden, and the fireflies at night.

Sarah was glad Alex was with her; she knew that if she'd been alone and heard that awful buzzing sound, she'd have given up and gone inside. Still, the dread of that buzzing made her skin prickle.

"Maybe your grandpa can help us," Alex asked. "With the sword." He didn't seem bothered by the noise, even as it grew louder and louder, filling the wide blue sky and all the treetops.

"I guess." Sarah was less keen on making it now. The splinter still hurt in her finger.

"After we make it, can I keep it here at your house?" asked Alex.

Sarah didn't understand.

"If Julian saw it, he'd probably smash it up," Alex answered. "He'd call me a dork, or worse."

Sarah could see it: Alex's brother would smash up the sword, break it into pieces and laugh. They'd have to be careful. More careful than they already were. Julian came over to hang out with Sarah's brother sometimes, and whenever he saw Sarah and Alex playing, he'd scowl, and then Jay and he would snicker to themselves.

Sarah knew she was a "dork" or "loser" to Julian. Maybe even to Jay too. But when she watched Alex's face, after the sneers and the vicious laughter, she knew it bothered Alex to be called those names. He still tried to play with the older boys. Still tried to be cool. Still wanted them to stop laughing.

Sarah wanted them to stop too, but she knew they'd never accept her, so she quit trying to make nice and worm her way into their orbit. She knew that no little sister was welcome in such company, even if Jay did play with her sometimes, when it was just the two of them, in the house, away from the yells and scowls of Julian and Jaime.

Alex wanted to be welcomed; maybe because he was a boy, or maybe because he wasn't like Sarah. And he knew, and she knew, that a homemade wooden sword was the kind of thing that would set Julian off. He'd snap it like a twig, gleeful in his act of destruction.

"You can keep it here," replied Sarah. "But we need a good place to hide them."

The buzzing grew louder and louder. Sarah's eyes started to drift toward the edge of the woods, searching for the source of the cacophony. It was late afternoon, the sun off in the western sky, and the forest was dark with growing shadows. Sarah recalled the evening when she imagined the faerie knight. Could these sounds be coming from within the heart of the forest? From the borders of Avalon? Her blood ran cold and her skin prickled worse than ever.

"We got invited over for Fourth of July," said Alex, his voice cutting through the vibrating air. "Your grandma stopped by yesterday and my dad said yes."

"Your whole family?"

The boy nodded.

"That's okay. Maybe we can stay up real late and play ghosts-in-the-graveyard."

"Set off fireworks!"

Sarah shook her head. "I don't like fireworks. They scare me."

"Too loud?"

"No, it's the fire. People have horrible accidents with those, you know."

"Maybe, but only if you do something stupid."

"Setting off fireworks *is* doing something stupid."

"You're scared of everything," said Alex.

"No, I'm not! I didn't get scared when we hunted for crayfish the other day!"

"Yes, you did."

Sarah's face grew hot, her cheeks filling up with anger, shame, and annoyance all at once. She had been afraid, but only a little, and she didn't show it. She had waded into the water and forced a smile and even tried to grab for a few of the crayfish. It wasn't her fault she didn't catch any. How did Alex know she was scared?

"I don't like this buzzing," she said, standing up. "I'm going in."

"Okay. Let me know about the sword, alright?"

Sarah shrugged and sprinted into the house, leaving Alex alone on the lawn. The awful buzzing continued, but he'd had enough of it. His bike was leaning up against the garage, so he wandered over and straddled the crossbar. Just as he was about to pedal away, Alex stopped.

The creature on the pavement was unmissable: as long as his finger and thick-bodied, it looked like a giant fly, a laboratory experiment gone wrong, or an alien insect from another planet. It lay on its back, wings tucked under its frozen body. As Alex came closer, he expected it to fly away, but it didn't. Rigid as a corpse, the giant winged bug just lay there, unmoving.

Alex wanted to get closer, to lean down and see what kind of bug it really was, but something stopped him. He wasn't afraid, but he wasn't sure he wanted to get too close. Something about its stillness unnerved him. Nothing alive should be that still. But if it was dead, its death was a mystery. It wasn't squashed or smashed; it wasn't injured. It was just there, in the middle of the driveway, lying on its back. Helpless. Exposed.

Alex felt a prickle along the back of his neck. His mind conjured a million things at once. What if he knelt and the bug sprang to life? What if it was poisonous? What if it flew right at him, into his eyes, attacking his face, stinging his skin? What if it started to move, and it followed him home, and it landed on his back as he sped away on his bike? What if it was still there on the pavement tomorrow, in the same spot, unmoved and unmoving?

That was the worst thought of all. That it could lay there all day and all night and all the next day, and never move, but still be alive. Waiting for something or nothing. Just waiting.

Alex wanted to step on it and kill it, end its existence, but he couldn't. His legs were welded to the bike pedals. His mind raced again, this time filling up with Julian's words. *Pussy. Dweeb. Dork. Loser.*

Alex pushed the pedals of his bike, struggling against inertia, willing his wheels forward. The front tire crunched over the body of the bug, breaking it into a hundred fragile pieces; exoskeleton, and antennae, and guts splattered the asphalt.

All around, the buzzing faded. The song ended. Alex pedaled, but he didn't go home. He rode around the neighborhood, hoping the yellow ichor on his tires would eventually rub off.

CHAPTER TWELVE

Ghosts in the Graveyard

SOMEONE CRIED OUT: "Ghost in the graveyard, run, run, run!" A firecracker lit and screamed into the sky. Ice cream and strawberry pie melted on a paper plate. The grill had been turned off hours ago, but the smell of charred hot dogs and burgers still hung in the air.

Sarah ran as fast as her legs could carry her; she wasn't safe yet. Out of the corner of her eye, she saw Julian Guerrera charging for her, his wolfish eyes hungry for a victim. She was heaving heavy gulps of air. Not enough. The ghost slammed a hard palm on her back, and she tripped, rolled in the grass, a heap.

"Ha!" cried the ghost, and Julian stood over her in triumph.

"You're supposed to tag everybody, not just me." Sarah stood up, wincing at the scratches on her knees.

"Everybody else is safe. You're just slow."

Sarah's face grew hot and red, but in the dusky night, Julian couldn't see.

"Fine."

"You're the new ghost."

"I *know*." Sarah started up the hill without looking back at the older boy.

They returned to the big oak tree in front of the house.

"He got you?" asked Alex.

Sarah nodded. Another firecracker whistled into the air and exploded into green showers.

"Start counting. I'm hungry to harvest more ghosts," said Julian, grinning. The others—Jay and Jaime, Alex, Mrs. Fabrizio's grandkids, Uncle Jim's nephew Mark—all stood catching their breath by the tree. They closed their eyes and started the countdown.

"One o'clock, two o'clock, three o'clock…"

Julian turned quickly and growled at Sarah. "Don't follow me."

She didn't want to. Sarah hated being "it" with Julian. No matter what the rules of the game might say, they were *not* a team. Sarah would find her own hiding place and hope the others might forget about her.

Even though it was dark, and the forest loomed all around them like some vast, encroaching gloom, Sarah wasn't afraid. There was too much commotion, too much noise from the fireworks.

No matter where she looked or what sounds she could hear, Sarah felt safe. Even Julian and the other older kids weren't going to bother her tonight; too many adults lingered at the edges of the house, under the awning, near the picnic tables, around the lawn.

The energy of the party electrified even the fireflies as they danced above the grass. Sarah felt that wonderful feeling of being home, of knowing that the world was warm and the summer was endless. It had been a long time since she'd felt that way; she could hardly remember feeling it at all in California.

Julian was gone before she knew it. She could hear the others getting close to counting midnight, so she fled to the far side of the house, away from the picnic tables and sparklers. She was near the edge of the forest now, near the sloping valley below her grandparents' house and the creek that ran through it. The path that led into the woods wasn't far.

Sarah remembered the rusted gates.

Only a few days into summer, she remembered pulling Alex along into the sun-drenched woods. She had backed away from the gates that day, her heart faltering. She hadn't been ready.

But now, in the darkness of a sweltering summer night, she felt differently. Somewhere in that small patch of woods, the rusted gates waited to be opened. Sarah knew they would unlock the way to Avalon. Hadn't the book said so?

The book. *Gates to Illvelion* by A.R. Rathmann.

When Sarah brought the book home from the Book Depot, she didn't start reading it right away. She had stared at the cover, wondering. The iron gates were just like the ones she and Alex had found. It was as if the artist who drew the illustration had once looked at the same forest, the same clearing, the same rusted gates.

Sarah had stared at that cover for a long time, her eyes tracing every line, every detail. She lingered on the white unicorn, who seemed to be looking right back at her. She tried to search out the tree branches and undergrowth that would identify this forest clearing as her forest clearing. Seeking, gazing, she yearned for some clue, some sign.

At last, she had opened the book to the first chapter: "Faerie Night."

The words made her shiver a bit, even in the hotness of her summertime bedroom. When her eyes finally began their journey across the pages, she had felt things at once strange and familiar.

The book began on a dark summer night, warm and filled with fireflies. Lord Agravaine and his daughter had come to find the fairies on the border of their realm, along the edges of the vast, ancient forest. The fairies and wild folk always lived along the edges of things. It was on that dark night that Lord Agravaine was stolen away, into the wonder-world of Illvelion, and his daughter was left bereaved and resolved to find her father once more. Thus the adventure began.

Sarah made sure not to read too much or too quickly. She wanted the book to last. There was excitement in her reading, yet a kind of dread too, as if something lay within the story that she wasn't quite ready to face. But Sarah had read enough to know that the key nestled in her pocket was the iron key that would open the gates.

That had been a week ago. Now Sarah stood upon the edge of her grandparents' forest and couldn't help but remember the words of the book.

Fireworks exploded. Laughter and happy screams echoed down into the darkened valley. Sarah heard them, but that world seemed so far away. Instead, she kept her gaze fixed upon the forest.

Was she waiting for the fairies to appear? Would they steal her away just as they had done Lord Agravaine?

If she crossed the threshold into the forest, would she arouse the attention of the nine queens? Or perhaps something worse.

Somehow, Sarah's own stories and make-believe were mingled with the tale told in the paperback book, and all of it started to feel possible, as if A.R. Rathmann, and the bookshop clerk, and whoever put those rusted gates into the clearing all knew that something was real within that forest. Something magical.

She stepped closer to the borders of the dark wood. She felt the tree branches quiver when suddenly a strong breeze swept through them. She saw strange shadows in the gloom.

And then a tall figure moved, a shadow come to life.

Sarah's stomach leaped into her throat. She didn't dare move. Whatever it was in the forest was moving toward her, as surely as the moon rises high on a summer's night. The figure was tall, taller than a mortal man, but slim, like a sapling sprung from the earth.

Sarah wanted to run—she knew that she should—but fear kept her frozen. Slowly the figure moved, like seaweed in water, but there was no mistaking its movement toward her.

The fairies? A ghost? Or worse?

Sarah wanted to cry and yell for help, but she couldn't. She was rooted to the spot and at the mercy of the figure stalking slowly through the trees.

The fireworks screamed above her, exploding into rain-fire of green and blue. Cheers and shouts went up from the people on the hill.

Then a child cried, "Ghosts in the graveyard! Run, run, run!" and the figure in the woods stopped, seized with its own fear. Like a startled deer or rabbit, it fled back into the heart of the forest. Sarah saw it run with long leaps and bounds, a man on stilts or a denizen of Faerie. She thought she saw a glint of silver flash from its body as it ran.

Up above, the children scattered and screamed as another

ghost was made and taken to the oak tree in front of the house. Sarah ran after the noise, glad to be in the warmth of the summer lanterns again. She smiled at the white-hot light of sparklers and the face of Alex as he stood safe next to the big oak. Already the thing she'd seen upon the edge of the woods was fading from her mind. Only imagination, nothing more.

Julian's eyes caught her as she came near. "The loser returns," he sneered.

"Where'd you hide?" Jay asked. "We looked everywhere."

Sarah told them she had gone down into the valley. "I didn't really hide. Just stood near the woods."

"That's brave!" one of Mrs. Fabrizio's grandchildren said.

Sarah didn't answer.

"I looked down there," said Jay. "I didn't see you."

"I was pretty far down," answered Sarah. "Right near the trees."

"Play again?" Jaime asked.

"Naw, I'm done," said Julian. "Kiddie stuff anyway." He slouched away from the others and headed off to make mischief. Jay and Jaime soon followed.

"Sore loser," said Alex softly when the older brothers had gone. "He couldn't catch anybody."

"He caught me," Sarah reminded.

"But you didn't really play either, did you?"

"Alex—"

"Yeah?"

"I saw something—"

"What do you mean?"

Sarah couldn't say. What would she say, after all? That she'd seen a fairy in the woods and he'd almost stolen her away? No.

"What did you see?" Alex asked again.

"Nothing. Just the forest. Gave me the creeps."

"You're getting braver. You wouldn't have gone near the forest at night when summer began."

Sarah realized Alex was right. *What had changed?* she wondered.

"Well," Sarah began, "I won't go near it again at night. Not alone, anyway."

"It's just a bunch of trees. Same at night as in the day. Maybe more raccoons." Alex smiled, his dark eyes glinting in the house lamps.

Sarah smiled too, but it was slight and forced. As much as she tried to pretend it was her imagination, she knew that the thing in the forest was more than a raccoon. And it was that thought which made her shiver again: the thought of what lay beyond the trees and the rusted gates and the border of her world.

CHAPTER THIRTEEN

Candy and Magazines

THE METRONOME CLICKED its incessant rhythm. Alex's hands hovered over the keys. He tried to concentrate, staring hard at the black dots on the music sheet. Tried to focus.

But the yelling. The yelling was louder, even though his dad had closed the bedroom door. Alex tried to block out the words, focus on the music, listen to the metronome. There were moments of silence when the person on the other end of the phone must have been talking. And then the yelling again. Alex's fingers hovered. He tried to see the notes through blurred eyes. He knew he should push down and strike the key, start the music, block out everything else. Instead, the metronome played its own steady, rigid song.

"Your mother is working late tonight," said his dad. He'd come out of the bedroom. Sat on the couch. "Play something for me?" Alex's dad tried to smile. He wiped his brow from sweat or from worry, but Alex thought his father looked a hundred years older suddenly, shadows and lines filling all the pockmarks and crevices of his weary face.

"I just finished practicing," Alex lied. "My fingers are kinda tired."

"Oh." His father looked down into his own folded hands. "That's fine."

"Can I go to the Rays' house?"

"Eh?" His father's eyes were far away. He wouldn't have heard the song even if Alex had played for him. "Right. Yeah, sure."

The metronome was silenced. Alex slid off the piano bench and walked toward the kitchen.

"Will you be home for dinner?" his dad asked.

"I'll try. Unless Mrs. Ray makes me stay."

"She probably will." His dad sighed. "Better that way. You'll get a good meal."

Alex wanted to say, "You're a good cook too!" He wanted to smile for his father and reassure him. He wanted to sit back down at the piano and play the song that he should have played earlier.

But he didn't. Instead, he waved meekly and turned to go.

"Hold up, wuss." Julian had been hovering, waiting just outside the back door. He shoved Alex in the shoulder as soon as the younger boy had stepped onto the backyard pavement. "We're going to the bookstore."

Alex knew this was no literary excursion. In his brothers' minds, the books were only incidental. What they really wanted were dirty magazines, maybe swipe some candy. Petty thievery. A chance to get out of the house and away from their catatonic dad.

"I'm going to Sarah's."

"Naw, you're coming with us."

"Yeah, little bro," said Jaime. "We need a lookout."

Even though Jaime was the oldest brother, he deferred to Julian. Maybe it was because he was shorter and pudgier than his younger brother, or maybe it was to make up for his success in school. Jaime had always gotten straight A's. He never had to worry about tests or homework. It all came so easily to him.

But for young teenage boys like Jaime or Julian, being good at school was something to keep hidden, something to keep quiet. So Jaime let Julian take the lead, let him be the boss. Jaime always stepped back and gave Julian the power. Maybe it was fear, or maybe it was embarrassment. Either way, Alex knew he had no ally in his oldest brother.

"Outta my way," Alex replied, pushing past Julian to get to his bike.

"Whoa! Check out the big balls on this cabrón!" Julian smiled derisively. "When did you grow a pair, little bro?"

Anger welled up in Alex. He didn't have patience for Julian's bullying or his taunts. There was something building inside of Alex, a rage and helplessness that he couldn't control. He wanted to scream or to cry or to run, and if his brothers got in his way, then perhaps he would fight too.

"Come on, Julian, let him go." Jaime's half-hearted attempt to cool things down failed as usual.

"Naw, I wanna see this new tough guy we got here." Julian stalked over to Alex's bike and blocked the way. "You feeling some heat, bro?"

Alex gritted his teeth. "Just let me go to Sarah's."

"Aw! Need some comfort, eh? Your girl gonna suck you off—"

Alex exploded. His fist shot out like a piston, ramming Julian in the chest.

It must have hurt the older boy, but Julian barely showed

it. He kept the derisive grin on his face, but his eyes burned white hot.

"Gotta work on that right hook. Or maybe get your girlfriend to give you her sword."

Tears streamed out of Alex's eyes now. He gripped the handlebars of the bike and tried to pedal away, but Julian shoved him in the shoulder again, knocking him down. Dirt and blood streaked across Alex's knee.

"Alright, now that you've learned your lesson, let's get going to the bookstore." Julian and Jaime both got on their bikes. Alex wiped tears and blood, picked up his own bike, and followed.

Just as the three started pedaling down the driveway, they heard a voice shout from behind.

"Wait up!"

It was Sarah, riding her bike.

"It's your knight in shining armor," Julian said grinning that horrible grin.

Alex didn't look Sarah in the eye when she caught up with them. He rode along in silence letting her chatter away.

"I'M on chapter six now. 'Gallien, the Unicorn.' It's really good."

Alex was barely listening. Sarah hadn't stopped talking about the book she'd been reading, about how it reminded her of some of their adventures, and how it made her feel like the author knew some secret that would change everything.

"It's like he's seen our forest and the gates and everything. Like there's something in the woods that might be real."

"You mean the trees?" Alex mumbled.

Sarah shook her head. "No, I mean something magical."

Alex tried to ignore her. He put his head down and picked up a nearby magazine. It was one of those humor magazines with comics and spoofs and crass jokes.

"That's the one, little bro." Julian was next to him suddenly, whispering. "Stick it down your pants while that lard-ass bookstore guy isn't looking."

Sarah's eyes said "no." But Alex looked away. He glanced at the sales counter. The bookseller wasn't there. Searching the store, Alex saw no sign of the stout man. He looked back down at the magazine. A grinning cartoon face stared back at him, its rows of white teeth looking like piano keys. As quickly as he could, Alex rolled up the magazine and stuffed it down his mesh shorts, covering the bulge as best he could with his oversized t-shirt.

Luckily, the magazine racks were right near the entrance. Only a few steps and he would be free. He didn't look back; head down and resolute, he walked out of the store. He didn't even wait to see if Sarah had followed.

A few moments later, Julian and Jaime came out too, laughing and high-fiving. Jaime quickly opened his closed fists and showed Alex the candy cigarettes he had palmed. Julian nodded at Alex and gave him a playful slug in the arm.

"Nice work, cabrón."

The older boys straddled their bikes and started to pedal away. Alex stopped, though, and looked back at the bookstore. He watched for Sarah as his brothers cycled through the parking lot. He waited for what felt like a long time, but she never came out.

Suddenly, a panic came over him. What if the bookseller had stopped her? What if he thought she was stealing too?

Alex tried to grip the handlebars of his bike, but his hands were shaking. The magazine was still stuck in his pants, the paper starting to stick to his sweaty skin.

He had to go. Now, now, now. But he couldn't move. His feet were leaden.

Why didn't she come out?

"Come on, dickwad!" called Julian. He and Jaime were almost out of the shopping center parking lot.

He had to go. He forced his feet to push down on the bike pedals, keeping his eyes focused on his brothers in the distance. It felt like the asphalt paving had thickened to heavy tar, but that was only because Alex was still shaking. And the magazine under his clothes made it awkward to ride.

They rode on and on, past the main road and into a nearby subdivision. Then they cut between two houses, riding over a weathered trail of brown grass, and into the gravel path that skirted along a small patch of woods. This little wilderness was nothing like the larger wood that edged its way up to their backyard and surrounded the Ray house far behind their own. But seeing the trees here made Alex think of Sarah again. His side hurt, like a cramp that came from running too hard. But he wondered if this cramp came from pedaling or from something else.

"I didn't think you'd do it," said Julian. His voice had changed, Alex could tell. The sneer was gone, replaced by affability.

"Hell yeah!" Jaime beamed at Alex. "What'd you grab?"

"I dunno. The kind with all the movie spoofs and stuff."

"Rad!"

"I guess." But Alex's cramp was getting worse. He realized they would have to head back home now. What would his dad say when he came into the house? He'd mention Sarah and Grandma Ray and Alex didn't want to face it. "Maybe we can ride around for a bit?" His voice was weak, barely a squeak.

"Naw, I wanna go check out my haul." Julian grinned.

Alex didn't see Julian come out of the store with anything. What was his haul?

"Yeah, dude, you never showed me what you got!" Jaime said, reading Alex's mind.

"You'll see." Julian winked and curled his lips up into what he must have thought was a sly smirk.

All the excitement, all the thrill of their escapade faded away. Julian had probably stolen some dirty magazine or a pack of baseball cards or a gun catalog. It all felt so stupid now. Why had Alex done it?

And Sarah was left there alone. He hadn't even said goodbye.

"WHERE DID YOUR COMRADES GO?" The bookseller glared at Sarah from behind his spectacles. The man wore the same white shirt and suspenders that he'd been wearing last time when he'd given her *Gates to Illvelion*.

Sarah had been frozen to her spot after Alex put the magazine down his pants. She couldn't believe it. He hated Julian! And now he was stealing magazines with him. Sarah must have been standing there for a long time because when the bookseller finally came over, she realized that Alex and the others were gone.

"I—" she began. "They left."

"That is becoming plainly obvious. But why are you still here?"

Sarah had no good answer. She wasn't looking for a book,

not really. *Gates to Illvelion* was more than she could handle at the moment.

"That book you gave me..." she started.

"Gave you?"

"I mean the one you picked out for me... *Gates to Illvelion.*"

She saw the bookseller's eyebrows raise slightly. "Yes?"

She had too many questions, and all of them sounded ridiculous now as she tried to formulate the words. "What about the author?" she blurted out.

"What about the author?" the bookseller repeated.

Sarah stammered. She wanted to ask who the author might be, whether he could possibly know her woods or some secret about the gates or anything. "Just, well, I mean... Who is he?"

"A. R. Rathmann? A spinner of yarns. A teller of tales. What more needs be said?"

Sarah felt stupid. She said no more.

But as she turned to go, the bookseller's voice stopped her.

"To be more precise, no one knows who A. R. Rathmann is. Never saw a publicity photo. No interviews ever given. Most likely the name is a pseudonym."

Sarah didn't know what that meant.

"It means A. R. Rathmann is a made-up name. It means the real author could be anyone."

Anyone? Sarah's stomach suddenly filled with butterflies. She wasn't sure why. Why did it matter that A. R. Rathmann was a made-up name?

It wouldn't have mattered to her grandmother or grandfather, or Jay, or Alex even, but somehow it mattered to her. Somehow, the mystery of it mattered.

~

THEY RODE past Mr. Henderson's house and saw the old man wheeling his toilet out to the garbage. He had it in a wheelbarrow, and then, straining to lift it, he dumped it by the side of the road. Alex could see the exhaustion on the old man's face. Pedaling ahead, Jaime and Julian cracked crude jokes and laughed at Henderson's sweaty, pained expression.

"Must've been some dump to break a toilet!" Julian crowed.

While the two boys snickered, Alex felt the eyes of Mr. Henderson glaring at him. It was as if the old man could tell, somehow, that Alex had done something wrong. Alex felt his face grow hot and red; he kept his eyes fixed on the back of his brothers' heads. But still, he could feel it, the judgment of Mr. Henderson, and the guilt in his own heart. He couldn't wait to get home just so he could throw the stolen magazine in the trash.

When they did arrive, Alex tried to slink off to his bedroom without letting his dad know he was home. But his dad was nowhere to be seen. All the lights were off and the house was quiet.

"No, no, no, little brother," Julian said, grabbing Alex's shoulder. "Come down to my lair and see forbidden wonders." His eyes promised more mischief.

Alex knew he couldn't say no.

The dirty magazine was flopped onto the old coffee table in the basement. Julian and Jaime both sat on the moth-eaten couch their dad had dumped down there when their mom decided to refurnish the living room a year ago. They hovered over the magazine like jackals, eyes shining and lips wet.

Alex stood behind the couch and caught a glimpse of the magazine's cover. His stomach lurched as he realized that within a few seconds, his brother would turn the pages and they'd probably see this same woman's naked breasts. Alex wasn't uncurious, but he also felt the wrongness of it: of stealing the magazine, of sneaking around behind their father's back.

"Julián!" It was Mr. Guerrera's voice shouting from upstairs. He always said the boys' names with the Spanish pronunciation; Julian hated the sound of the soft "j" in his name. "Julián!" their father continued. Although it was only one word, each of them could tell that their father's voice sounded slurred.

"He and mom had a fight on the phone," Alex said, sheepishly.

"You'd better go up, dude," said Jaime, though his face was pained.

Julian just shrugged. "Sure. I'll go up while you two sit down here and cry for mommy."

"What'd you do?" asked Jaime.

"Nothing. I ain't done nothing. Except Papi needs someone to blame, you know?"

The yelling and shouting between Julian and their dad went on for a long while. Alex couldn't go up but he didn't want to stay downstairs either. He just sat in a corner and flipped through the stupid magazine he'd stolen. He hated it but somehow he couldn't throw it away either. Looking at it was better than listening to the argument.

Jaime played video games on the old TV set they had hooked up.

Finally, the shouting stopped. Without another glimpse, Alex tossed the magazine aside and raced upstairs. Every light in the kitchen was turned on but no one was there. Alex listened for a moment to see if his dad would come in, but there wasn't any sign of either father or wayward son.

A small bit of daylight still clung to the sky outside, so Alex went through the back door to find solace in the yard. Maybe he was hoping to see Sarah ride by on her bike, or maybe Mr. Henderson would be out in his garden, and Alex could go over and help. But he was alone.

Toward the very edge of the Guerrera backyard, right before the woods began and the Rays' property started, there was a small oak that made for perfect climbing. The main trunk split in the middle and made two solid ladders that led up to the sturdy and plentiful limbs above.

Alex felt like climbing it, like reaching as high as he had ever dared. The mosquitoes were out in force and clouded around him as he first started up the tree, but soon he pushed himself higher and escaped their attacks, and found sure footing on the first rung of branches.

Higher and higher he went, pulling himself up so that soon he was standing higher than the roof of his house. At such a height, he was shrouded in foliage and could see all around the backyards and even the front yards of the neighbors.

Then he heard the screen door slam and someone stepped into his backyard. It was Julian.

Fuming and mumbling under his breath, Julian stormed through the yard and headed straight for the woods. Unnoticed on his bird-like perch, Alex watched as his older brother vanished into the underbrush of the forest.

Seconds later, Alex had scrambled down.

Where was Julian going?

Following as close as he dared, Alex tailed his brother through the woods. Julian seemed to be heading somewhere in particular; the determined way he stalked through the trees hinted that he knew where he was going and had been there before. Alex tried to keep close, but he worried that if he got too near, Julian would notice. So he hung back, hoping that he could listen and keep close to the sound of leaves crunching under Julian's feet.

But the tread of his brother's footsteps wasn't loud enough, and soon Alex lost the trail. He found himself in a part of the woods that was unfamiliar. He and Sarah usually stayed closer to the valley and creek down below the Rays' house; rarely did they venture into the flat and dense forest that stood on higher ground behind the houses of the neighboring subdivision.

It was hard to find a footpath through this part of the forest, and Alex worried he might not be able to make his way back to his own yard. He turned to retrace his steps, all the while wondering where Julian had marched off to.

It was then that he saw the man lying on the forest floor, his unmoving body leaning against a large tree trunk.

Alex blinked. *It couldn't be. Not like this.*

The man wore a shirt of linked chains under a tunic threaded in gold and ivory. His head was bare, but his hands wore gloves made of shimmering metal plates.

Gauntlets. That's what Sarah called them. Alex's breath caught in his throat. *A knight in armor.*

The man's eyes were closed and his head slumped, but the face wasn't pallid. Alex didn't dare move closer. Somehow, in some inexplicable way, he knew the man was still alive. He rubbed his eyes as if they had sand in them or the sun, but the vision persisted. The man in armor lay against the tree, asleep or else stricken.

The thought which crept into Alex's head made him shiver. It was the thought of Sarah's words and her stories, of the nine queens, of that place beyond the iron gates. Of the knight who had fallen into the magical sleep.

It was then that he read the image emblazoned upon the man's tunic, an image as familiar as the sunrise and as welcome as the rain. A tree grew from among the gold and ivory threads, a stout oak with branches that reached up to the sky. There, upon the man's chest, was an image of the forest, of summer, of green leaves canopied over the world. Across his heart, the image was sewn, as unmistakable as it was amazing. The very tree of life. A contrast to the sleeping figure who bore it.

The sun made its last hurrah, shining like an immense orange disk in the sky. The light caught Alex right in the eyes, and he squinted, losing sight of everything. He shielded his face and blinked, trying to blot out the kaleidoscope of colored dots that blurred his vision.

When at last the flash of color and light subsided, he tried looking again at the tree where the man lay. He was both afraid and determined. He would step closer, he told himself, he would.

And he did. But what he stepped toward was nothing. What he was afraid of was vapor. What he had seen was gone.

As Alex emerged from the woods into his backyard, he told himself over and over that it was just his imagination. There was no man, no tunic threaded with gold and ivory, no gauntlets, no magical sleep. Just Sarah's stories flooding into his head and Julian running off into the woods for who knows what, and his dad, and the magazines. And his mom.

But no man was lying there against the tree. It was just the sun in his eyes.

CHAPTER FOURTEEN

Twenty-Sided Dice

"I DON'T UNDERSTAND. Why did Mom send it to *you*?" Sarah was peering over Jay's shoulder as he set aside the box lid. Two twenty-sided dice rattled on top of the rulebook. They looked like nuggets of dragon gold.

"Because it's my birthday, duh."

Sarah decided it was incredibly unfair. She had been the one to ask for the game last Christmas, not Jay. And now it lay upon their grandparents' kitchen table—a glittering treasure —in her brother's possession.

"We can play together," he murmured.

But Sarah knew this wasn't true. Jay might let her watch, he might even think he was letting her play, but the game would really belong to the older brothers, to Jay and Julian and Jaime.

"Can I at least see the dice?"

Jay shrugged and made no attempt to impede her. Sarah's fingers curled around the hard plastic.

She'd never seen anything like them. Instead of dots, each side was marked with numerals. They felt heavier, more substantial than the ordinary dice from their ordinary board games. It was as if Jay had opened the tome of a long-dead magician and these dice were his arcane talismans.

A skeletal sorcerer-king with glowing red eyes adorned the cover of the rulebook. Sarah stared at the image, mesmerized by the danger and adventure it promised.

"When can we play?" She knew it was a fool's question, but the scent of the game had gotten into her now, the same musty, long-buried smell that her Uncle Jim's *Watchtower* game had promised, only this time, Sarah knew the promises would be kept. This game would be different.

"I dunno." Jay tossed the rulebook onto his bed and swung his legs onto the floor.

He jogged out of the room, and Sarah waited. She went over to the window and looked out, watching as Jay hopped on his bike and rode down the driveway toward the Guerrera house.

The rulebook beckoned. The ruby-crusted eyes of the sorcerer-king seemed to pulse with eldritch energy. Sarah knew it was just her imagination, but still, she wished it were true. She wished this rulebook, this game, might be the secret to finding Avalon. Or, at the very least, to having a real adventure.

Reaching under her bed, she pulled out the brown shoebox that held her hoard of treasures: the Carolingian coins from Mrs. Fabrizio, the paperback copy of *Gates to Illvelion*, the skeleton key from her grandfather's toolbox.

She placed the speckled twenty-sided dice beside the others and closed the lid. With the treasure box under one arm and the rulebook under the other, Sarah dashed down the stairs. The sun blazed outside. July was reaching its zenith.

Secret games must be played in secret places. Sarah ran from the house, and all the while, her neck tingled from nervous energy. Jay was gone, but she still worried: *What if he should come back?*

She went down the hill away from the house, heading toward the forest. Deep in the woods was the fox's headstone and the abandoned barn and all those fallen logs that reminded her of giants' bones, but Sarah needed someplace even more secret. She also worried about what lurked in that part of the woods, ever since the fireworks exploded and she saw a shadow of something less than human.

She followed along the edge of the creek that separated the valley from the woods and headed toward a place that she and Alex had never explored. This eastern part of the forest was denser, choked with thorny bushes, and with no clear path to follow.

Sarah picked her way through the underbrush while raspberry branches scratched at her clothes and skin. The wild berries were everywhere, dotting the green landscape like pricks of bright blood.

The creek stayed ever in her sight so that she might find her way back, but all the while, Sarah thought of the ruby-eyed sorcerer and Gallien the unicorn, and stories from her head mingled with stories from her books.

She imagined the hutch of the Troll-Hag and saw the veiled faces of the nine queens, but even as she spun such stories, the tall, shadowy figure from the Fourth of July kept creeping into her head.

He was an intruder to her stories, worse than the queens and their enchantments. His face was sometimes a mask of darkness, but now he took on the visage of the skeletal sorcerer from the role-playing game. Her eyes began to play tricks on her; every tree and branch held the willowy image of the intruder. Every sound was his footsteps.

Sarah held the treasure box tight against her body, while her hands grew sweaty as they grasped the rulebook. She looked often at the creek, but by this time the house and the driveway and all the familiar things were gone. Dense woods surrounded her on every side.

Was this place secret enough?

Sarah did not stop. She delved deeper.

The creek started to widen and the water flowed faster. The ground began to slope downward, and Sarah could see a clearing up ahead. She wondered what Alex might say about her adventure. Would he believe it? Sarah could hardly understand what made her keep going, for she felt both fear and wonder in equal measure, and yet she could not turn back.

A word drifted through her head, and she couldn't get it out. At first, it was as small as a mouse's whisper, but then it became something more sure and startling.

Enchantment.

Sarah's feet kept moving even as her skin prickled with growing uncertainty. She couldn't stop herself. She had to keep going, had to find out what was in that clearing, had to read the rulebook and play the game. Was she enchanted? Is this what had happened to the Oak-Hearted Knight? Was he put under a spell and forced to travel into the heart of Avalon only to be put into a deep and unending slumber?

Sarah knew these were just stories; she kept telling herself these were just stories. But the figure of the strange intruder, the dark shadow of that night when the fireworks blazed the sky, he had been real, she was sure of it now. He had been real, and she could feel his presence even in these unvisited woods.

She stepped out of the dense trees and into the clearing. The creek here opened into a wide, rocky ford that spanned several yards, and on the right bank of the ford, a cliff of muddy clay towered over the lowland.

The forest stretched off to the right and seemed to lead to higher ground. If she went back into the woods and followed the incline, Sarah decided she could reach the top of the cliff.

But here at the bottom, where the water danced over rock and clay, and the muddy walls of the cliffside were as gray as slate, Sarah knew she had found her secret place. The whole thing reminded her of something she seemed to know, like a vision from a dream.

Then the box under her arm tugged at her memory, and she felt that same eerie and excited feeling as when she'd first beheld the cover of *Gates to Illvelion*.

She sat down on a patch of grass and opened the shoebox, drawing out the book as fast as she could. The rulebook of the role-playing game fell from under her arm and landed on the ground, forgotten in her haste to open the box.

She took out the paperback and flipped through its pages until she found the chapter she was looking for. There in black and white were the words she had only half-remembered, but now all of it came flooding back.

The stream here had diminished into a smaller rivulet, and looming above her was the silver-gray cliffside covered in wet clay.

Sarah read the words over and over, and the image which formed in her mind was the same as that which she could now see with her eyes.

The cliffs were here, right here in this clearing, as real as the book she held in her hand. But how could a book—a mere story—tell her something so real? How could this cliff exist in both the pages of her paperback and in front of her very eyes?

As she wondered about all this, something moved atop the cliff. It was unmistakable. A human shape, but stretched and misshapen. There was someone there, someone peering down at her.

Sarah's stomach leaped into her throat. She remembered suddenly that she was all alone in a strange part of the forest. Panic filled every bone in her body. She tried to move—her first instinct was to run—but she couldn't. She sat motionless, bewitched by fear. The stranger was looking at her; she knew it, even though she couldn't quite see him.

Then he moved, scurrying like a badger down the pebbled hill, and Sarah felt her muscles loosen at last. She threw the book back into her treasure box, slammed the lid down on the precious contents, and ran.

She ran without a thought of Avalon or the nine queens or Gallien or the Mud Lord. All stories melted from her and fled into the ground. Her only desire was to run, to flee, to be back home. She ran so hard and so fast that the raspberry thorns tore at her bare legs and streaked them red. But still, she ran, holding tight to her shoebox and never looking back.

When Julian had come down from the hill and stood by the shallow creek, he laughed a little to himself. He hadn't meant to scare Alex's dorky friend, but it was better this way. This clay-streaked cliff was his discovery, his domain.

At first, he didn't notice what she'd left behind, but when he turned to go back up the hill, his foot slid across a wide, slim book adorned with the face of a skeletal sorcerer.

Julian wanted to scoff at it—more of Alex and Sarah's lame fantasy crap—but something held him back. This book was different. The creature on the cover looked dangerous.

He picked it up and leafed through the pages. The charts and maps and text looked like an arcane language. With a satisfied shrug of his shoulders, he tucked the book under his arm and loped back up the hill.

~

"Check this out." Julian threw the rulebook down on the basement couch. "It's some kind of game."

"Hey, that's mine!" Jay looked up from the video game screen and snatched up the book. "What the hell, man?"

"I didn't know. Quit yer crying." Julian flopped down on the couch next to him and picked up Jay's controller. "I got next game."

"Bring it on," said Jaime, hitting "restart." The video game's intro music clambered to life.

While the two brothers chose their fighters and prepared for a virtual kung-fu battle, Jay leafed through the pages of his birthday present.

"It says something about needing twenty-sided dice," said Julian as his video game avatar pummeled Jaime's into a bloody pulp.

"Yeah," Jay mumbled. "Sarah has them, I guess." He didn't look at Julian.

"Look, dude, I found it. It was just laying in the dirt out in the woods."

"Really?"

"Yeah, dude. I dunno how it got there."

Jay was starting to know. He remembered the longing in his sister's eyes.

"Anyway, it looks pretty cool." Julian shrugged again and didn't dare look directly at Jay or the book. He kept his eyes just a little too focused on the video game screen.

"It's a lot to read," said Jay.

"Yeah."

Jaime glanced at it. "How does it work? I mean, is there a board or pieces?"

"I think you need to write stuff down. Maybe draw maps. There's no board," Jay answered.

"That's weird."

"It might be okay," Julian said, this time unable to hide his eagerness.

"Sure. I guess I'll take a look," said Jay. "Maybe play tomorrow?"

"We gotta get the dice."

Jay nodded. He remembered promising Sarah that she could play too. Part of him was angry; she had taken his book and lost it in the woods. But part of him was guilty; Sarah had been the one to want the game in the first place. Their mother had screwed up.

Not a big surprise, thought Jay. Anne Lewis was supreme at screwing up. Even when she tried to do something nice, it ended up ruined. His birthday had been three days ago, and yet she'd never even called. Jay knew she'd call eventually and give some excuse about the shooting schedule and the call times and how hard it was being an actress, and he'd reassure her that everything was okay and not to worry. It didn't really bother him, not much. He was used to his mom's habits.

But Sarah was different. She would shoot layups and tell her stories and think that no one noticed when she talked to herself under her breath. She was clueless and way too trusting. When their mom sent a too-late birthday present that was all wrong and unintentionally thoughtless, Sarah wouldn't be able to shrug it off the way Jay could. She would feel it.

"I gotta go," he said, standing up.

"Already, man?"

"Yeah. I mean, if I'm gonna read this stupid rulebook, I better get started."

"Sweet, dude. We'll come over tomorrow."

Jay nodded and headed to the surface, leaving Julian and Jaime to finish their 16-bit duel.

~

SARAH DIDN'T GO BACK to her grandparents. When she got close to the house, she saw Alex riding his bike down the driveway.

"Alex!" She ran after him.

When he heard her, he stopped and pedaled back. "You okay?"

She was breathless. "Something... I saw something."

Alex thought suddenly of his own strange vision: the man lying against the tree, the knight sleeping in the woods. He said nothing.

"A man, or something like a man," Sarah continued, her breathing starting to slow. "I'm not sure."

"Not sure?"

Sarah realized this wasn't like what she had seen on the Fourth. Standing in the open air and sunshine with Alex made her accept the encounter by the cliff for what it was. Ordinary. Mundane.

"Probably a neighbor hiking through the woods," Alex said. "Your grandparents aren't the only ones who live around here, you know."

His explanation made sense. Sarah found herself nodding in agreement. "You're right. I guess I was just overreacting."

"Big surprise," said Alex, smiling.

"Shut up." Sarah pretended to scowl but ended up smiling too.

"Let's go get slushies."

"I gotta stash this!" said Sarah, running up the hill with her treasure box under her arm.

A few minutes later, the two of them rode through the subdivision toward the patch of trees that separated the houses from the fields behind the middle school. As their bikes broke into the clearing, they saw the huge brick building in the distance.

The sun was the whole sky, bright and yellow, one hundred million flames bursting across the atmosphere, and the heat was the air all around them, heat upon the grass and the trees and the paved bike path and the children who rode there, and when they came closer to the school, they could see the air around the school quivering with heat so that even the shadows on the brick walls were made of dark flame.

Sarah's face was flushed and dampened by sweat. She stopped her bike and looked at the empty school. The asphalt parking lot was like a prehistoric tar pit, and Sarah wondered if the rubber of her tires would melt when she rode across.

The school looked like a fortress, long-abandoned or dormant now because the ghosts inside were biding their time. It seemed impossibly big: two stories, sprawling, massive. The windows were dark. Nothing like Sarah's elementary school, the one in California that had so many open windows and pictures taped on them and classrooms that were bursting with books and art and color. This place— the middle school—was an inscrutable monolith, a void. Despite the heat, Sarah sensed that it was cold within.

Alex stopped his bike next to her. He pointed to the sign: HAVE A GREAT SUMMER! SEE YOU NEXT YEAR!

"Do you think you'll still be here when school starts?" Alex asked.

The sun painted everything around her a bright yellow. "I don't think so," replied Sarah, shielding her eyes.

"When will you know?"

Sarah didn't. She wasn't ready for middle school or the end of summer or California.

No. She was ready for the sun to melt her into a puddle, for the pool water to cool her, for running through the sun-dappled forest, for rolling those twenty-sided dice and delving down into the tomb of the sorcerer-king...

Oh, no. No, no, no.

"I gotta go," she said, panic in her voice. Her head hurt and her chest tightened as it flooded with guilt. She had just now remembered the book—her brother's birthday present—dropped on the rocky ground by the mud cliff.

Turning her bike, she sped back toward the subdivision, abandoning Alex to the emptiness of the parking lot. Muscles aching, Sarah tried to remember the path she took into that unfamiliar part of the woods.

"Stay close to the creek," she muttered under her breath. It was the only way.

Soon, her grandparents' house loomed, but Sarah pedaled faster. Jay's bike was already leaning against the garage. She prayed he hadn't yet discovered her theft.

Down in the valley, an army of walking skeletons stood waiting for her. They had come to punish the wicked thief.

It's the heat, it's the heat. It's my head hurting.

Their eyes glowed red, like dark rubies, and their jaws dropped as if silently screaming. Rusted swords, brittle halberds, spears eaten by ragged time: all these weapons they raised in defense of their un-dead master. The army stood guard upon the forest, and no one would pass. The way was blocked. Sarah would never regain what she had lost.

"Sarah!"

A hand reached out and touched her shoulder. She jumped out of her skin, and Jay snorted with laughter. He was behind her, doubled over in hysterics and holding the role-playing game in his hands.

"You went about ten feet in the air!" he said, still laughing. But once the laughter subsided, he spoke more gently. "I didn't mean to scare you."

Sarah didn't answer; she looked back down the valley and saw nothing but grass and ash trees. When she turned to her brother again, she noticed the role-playing game for the first time.

"How—?" she started.

"You said you wanted to play, right?" He held up the book and beamed.

Sarah nodded.

"Go get the dice."

"Jay, I thought—"

"Do you want to play or not?"

THE DICE WERE nuggets of dragon gold. They were a magic spell. They padded softly on the carpet floor.

Jay had barely skimmed the rules, so he made up a lot of it. Whenever he could, he had Sarah roll the dice. She relished every second. A high roll meant victory, a low roll defeat. Jay asked her lots of questions, and her answers made the world. She drew the world out of a million things: her books, her wanderings, her own wishes, her stories half-sketched in the twilight while shooting layups.

"It was like you gave me a gift," she said at last. "All of it. I saw everything that happened, every dungeon and cavern, all the wights and goblins. The dragon."

"The wizard." Jay grinned. He relished the memory. The wizard was more fearsome than any video game boss, and more real, despite being entirely imagined. Jay's thoughts lingered on the image of the skeletal necromancer, rising from the crypt to call forth his undead army. It was like being a little kid again and making up stories with his space soldier toys.

"I saw it happen, even though we never left this spot." Sarah's eyes were far away, still lost in the eldritch caverns.

"It worked then." Jay closed the rulebook.

"You tell a good story."

"I don't know. It was more your story than mine."

Sarah shook her head; she couldn't say anymore. The spell still lingered in the air and too many words would break it. At last, she said, "Will you play with Julian and Jaime?"

Jay shook his head. "I don't think they'd like it."

Sarah wondered. Maybe if they could all play then things would be different. Maybe they would be like true adventurers, brought together by fate and calamity, and in their travels and trials, a new bond would be forged. Maybe, if they could imagine a world together, they wouldn't be so far apart.

"Why don't you keep the dice?" Jay offered. "So they won't get lost."

Sarah wanted to hug him, but she didn't dare. Their family wasn't a family that hugged. She wasn't sure why. It was strange now that she thought of it. She'd never hugged her brother.

They both heard the phone ring downstairs, and their grandmother's voice called up. "Jay! Sarah! It's your mother!"

"She never completely forgets, does she?" Jay said to his sister.

"Mom?"

Jay nodded.

"No, not completely."

They hid the twenty-sided dice back in Sarah's shoebox and went downstairs.

CHAPTER FIFTEEN

Water Guns

For most of July, the pool was an oasis. On scorching days, when the heat chocked them, they could slip off their sweaty clothes and slide into new skin made of spandex, feel fish-like and lithe, then—skin prickling—submerge into an ice-cold chlorine bath, shocking their bodies with the temperature change, feeling tension and relief both at the same time.

Beyond the confines of the water, the heat enslaved, an oppressive overlord. But once the body met the water, once it dunked its head below the gleaming surface, it cooled. The heat no longer had power over it. On the high, hot days, the pool was a respite from unbearable heat.

But now, in waning summer, the pool had lost its luster. Games of Marco Polo had grown stale. Cannonball contests no longer inspired. Tubes and rafts had deflated, and no one had bothered to blow them up again. Something new was needed, something different.

Neon green and orange, bright cobalt blue, the Master Blaster was unlike any water gun they had ever seen before. It was the savior. No more pool-time boredom. Only war.

Sarah didn't have one, and Jay could only share what Julian

and Jaime allowed. The younger children were targets for extinction.

The older boys patrolled the perimeter of the house like sentries. They scanned the sheds and carport, keeping an eye on intruders. They watched for movement, for a blur of skin and neon t-shirts.

Sarah felt exposed and feeble holding the ordinary water gun. The trigger was hard to push down, sticking and jamming if she pushed too fast. She hadn't caught sight of Alex since the skirmish began. He'd been hit in the shoulder by Jaime's first volley and ran to the safety of the woods. Sarah almost joined him.

She hated games with guns. Too much fear, and not enough adventure. Give her a sword to swing, a foe to fight with dancing feet and happy strokes. But these guns could strike from any distance, it seemed, and Sarah hated the games of war. She tried to pretend they were space explorers on a distant planet and these water guns were laser pistols. The older brothers were the aliens. But the idea didn't make the game any less terrifying. Julian had vengeance in his eyes.

Hiding down below the house, Sarah was nestled into the wall of the stone staircase that led down to the walk-out basement. She listened for footsteps on the sidewalk above her. The quiet was almost more disturbing than hearing a noise. She knew she couldn't stay there forever.

I could just go in the house, she thought. *I don't have to play their stupid game.*

There was a streak of green and copper-colored skin, a boy's scream, something flying from the forest like a bat out of a private hell. The pursuer was bigger, a slump-shouldered menace. He wielded a Master Blaster.

Sarah couldn't abandon Alex to his fate. She ran after the

boys, up the hill, toward the front of the house. Alex was about to be pinned to the wall, his skinny body like one of those daddy longlegs that clung to the white stucco. Julian loomed over him, ready to empty his entire tank. Sarah knew she was still out of range, but she held her squirt gun up and called out to Julian. He didn't even turn around. He had found his target.

Alex's clothes, his face, his hair, every inch of him was soaked. Like a gangster with his Tommy gun, Julian sprayed the high-pressure stream of water all over his little brother.

Sarah was close enough now. She squirted her water gun at Julian, but the thin streams of water only made little raindrops on his black t-shirt. Alex was suffering, the water from the Master Blaster an endless torrent, so Sarah abandoned her feeble offense and leaped toward the wall to stand shoulder-to-shoulder with her friend. If he was to be destroyed, she would join him.

Julian laughed and turned his onslaught to Sarah. The water was frigid and stung as it struck her skin. Within seconds she was soaked, but it was nothing like being in the pool. It wasn't the freedom to float and feel weightless or to plunge into the depths and become a dolphin. The wetness from the Master Blaster was a soggy wetness, a coldness that never went away.

The tank on the massive water gun seemed bottomless. Julian kept laughing as Sarah and Alex became splat marks on the wall.

"You!" The voice barked from the doorway to the house. Grandpa Ray let the screen door clang behind him as he emerged, a scowl darker than any Sarah had ever seen. Julian didn't even notice the old man until it was too late. Like a hawk with its talons, Grandpa Ray snatched Julian by the ear and didn't let go. "Get the hell outta here, and take that contraption with you!"

With a shove, he released Julian's ear. The Master Blaster fell from Julian's hands, hitting the pavement with a hollow, plastic clang. The boy could barely look at the old man. Grandpa Ray's eyes cast fire. Even Sarah was frightened of him. Julian mumbled some kind of apology and then ran, taking his weapon with him. The plastic tank was scratched with jagged lines from where it hit the ground.

"You kids," Grandpa said, turning to the younger children, "go find your grandma for some new clothes." He almost turned around to go back inside, but a sudden thought made him stop. He looked down at the two frightened, soaking, shivering children and had a strange bout of pity. "After that," he continued, trying to be gentle, "come back to the garage."

Come back to the garage? Sarah didn't know what that meant. Were they going to be punished too? Would he make them sweep the floor or haul stuff to the carport? She and Alex sprinted off, skinny legs flying, first to the garden on the other side of the house, then to the clothesline hung between an oak tree and an iron pole, and finally into the living room where Grandma Ray was watching a soap opera and cutting coupons. She saw their sopping wet clothes and knew what to do.

Sufficiently dried and draped like mannequins in oversized t-shirts, the children shuffled outside toward the quiet garage. At first, they saw no one. Grandpa Ray's garage stood as it always did in the mid-afternoon: hot and empty and reeking of gasoline. Then the wooden stairs creaked.

Long ago, before Isabel or Anne were born, Joe Ray fixed up his garage by adding a second floor. A man could always use more storage, so Joe Ray added a sort of attic to his garage, a place to store sheets of plywood, two-by-fours, metal pipes, and whatever junk he might acquire over the years.

The stairs he built to access this loft were narrow, steep, and without any railing. Sarah never dared go up them because she was too afraid to come down. Too narrow, too steep. Nothing to help her keep steady.

Grandpa stood near the top of the stairs. "Get up here," he said, not unfriendly but still in that gruff way of his. Alex didn't hesitate, but Sarah's stomach clenched. Even after all these weeks, she still had her fears, and she hated that it was something as simple as a set of stairs that could make her feel powerless.

Once her foot was on the first step, she felt the narrowness of the space contract around her. It was like stepping into a shaft in an ancient pyramid, the crypt of the pharaoh waiting above.

"Come on," Grandpa Ray called from beyond the landing. Sarah couldn't see him or Alex; the angle of the steps prevented her from seeing much past the top stair.

Her hand reached out to hold the cinderblock wall, passing through a wispy cobweb that hung down from the corner of the garage. Sarah pulled away quickly, shaking the sticky web off, then wiping her hand on her shorts.

She looked at the cinderblocks again. No more cobwebs. She placed her fingers on the cold surface to keep herself steady.

She took one step up. The wooden stair creaked. Sarah felt woozy.

The stairs were just too steep.

"Come on, Sarah!" Alex's voice was eager. "You gotta see this!"

What was waiting for her at the top? Sarah tried to pretend that she was one of those rogues from Jay's role-playing game, that this was a wizard's tower and she was looking for arcane treasure. But the conceit didn't work. Her knees wobbled.

"Get your keister up here!" called Grandpa Ray.

Sarah leaned toward the wall; it was the only thing that could save her. She almost closed her eyes, but she didn't dare, or else she'd lose her balance. Her feet felt like they were wearing lead boots; each step made her stomach lurch. But as she moved up the staircase, toward the sunlit upper room of the garage, she felt herself getting lighter. Once she could see above the landing, see into the wide open space of that loft, she felt steadier.

She had made it. She clambered to the top landing, crawling the last bit with her hands before standing up. The whole loft was brightened by sunlight. Two windows, one at either end, filtered in the light. Dust motes danced across the beams. Junk was everywhere: two-by-fours, four-by-sixes, iron rods, flat boards of plywood, and PVC pipes. Piles of spare materials were sheltered under the eaves of the roof.

Grandpa Ray and Alex were standing at the far end, looking under the rafters at something deep in the recesses beneath the slanted ceiling.

"It's a submarine!" Alex blurted out before Sarah could even inquire.

Sarah thought she heard him wrong. It had to be something else.

"You heard him right," Grandpa Ray said to Sarah, reading her mind. A mischievous smile crossed his face. Sarah had never seen her grandfather smile like that.

She crept closer.

Resting in the darkness of the eaves was a lump of iron the size and shape of a fifty-five-gallon steel drum. Rudders and a propeller protruded from one end. A sail and two fins sat on top. Arising from the sail was a thin metal pipe capped with a lid and an oval pane of glass facing forward. Along the side of the barrel was a closed hatch door, barely large enough for someone to fit through.

"It works too," Grandpa continued. "At least, it used to."

"But—" Sarah began. She couldn't see how something like this could possibly work.

"Made it when I was just out of the service. Your grandmother thought I was crazy."

"It works? For real?" Alex said.

"Used to. Haven't tried it in forty-five years!"

All Sarah could think about was how her grandpa had managed to get that hunk of iron up those rickety, narrow steps.

"Could we?" Alex said, eyes glowing.

Grandpa Ray scratched behind his ear. "No place to use it, I'm afraid."

"The pool?"

"It'd scrape the lining."

"The creek?"

"Too shallow. This thing's gotta go deep."

Alex's face fell.

"I—" Joe Ray started. "Just thought you kids would like to see it."

"It *is* cool…" Alex's voice was flat.

Sarah thought it was more than cool. Looking at that hunk of iron and realizing that Grandpa Ray had mudded a real submarine—a working submarine—was incredible. He was some kind of genius.

She reached out and touched the hatch door. The cool, hard iron reminded her of the skeleton key hidden up in her secret shoebox.

And the gates in the woods.

"Come on," said Grandpa, patting the children on their shoulders. "Shoulda done this a long time ago."

Leading them back down the stairs, he grabbed a sheet of plywood and a few leather straps.

Going down was easier, somehow, for Sarah, than going up.

For the rest of the afternoon, the kids watched as Grandpa Ray cut the plywood into two round pieces and fastened the leather straps to each of the rounds.

"A shield!" Sarah cried when her grandfather held up his work.

"Not quite big enough, but if you crouch, those boys'll have a hard time soaking you again."

Sarah and Alex beamed.

Just before they turned to leave, Sarah stopped and faced her grandfather again.

"Grandpa?" she asked, voice low. Grandpa Ray was busy now with his tractor, his good deed done for the day.

"Eh?" Joe Ray tightened a screw and didn't look up.

"Remember that sword you made for me? The balsam wood one?"

"What about it?"

"Maybe you could…"

"Did you break it already?"

"No, I just meant—"

"Could you make one for me?" Alex said, coming to Sarah's aid.

"Eh?" Grandpa Ray stood up and wiped the grease off his

hands with a rag. "I suppose." He puttered around in the corner and found a couple of pieces that might work. "Am I showing you how it's done?"

Both children watched as he fastened the pieces together.

"There," said Joe Ray when he'd finished. "Now get along. Don't hit each other."

Sarah and Alex ran off into the backyard toward the creek. Julian and the older boys forgotten, their new shields firmly in hand, and Alex with his new sword swinging in the sunlight. They ran along the edge of the creek, following the dragonflies, and spotting goblins in the shadows of the forest.

Their games lasted all afternoon, and when their stomachs rumbled for dinner, and their sweaty skin needed cooling under the living room ceiling fan, they ran back to the house. They told tales of adventure, but Sarah never mentioned the nine queens of Avalon or the strange thing she saw in the forest, and Alex never mentioned the wounded knight. They kept their secrets to themselves.

When Alex ran home, he carried his sword and shield with him, all fear and danger forgotten.

CHAPTER SIXTEEN

Encyclopedias

ALICE REMEMBERED her father walking straight through her. Couldn't even see her. She didn't want to think the word.

Ghost.

No, just a man. He had merely looked like her father. Just a wandering hobo, a forgotten man. It had been 1938 after all.

Now it was 1992, early August, and when the young man in the brown suit came striding down the long driveway, Alice suddenly remembered that day when she was ten, when the cancered man appeared out of nowhere in the field and walked right through her. His suit had hung loosely off his shriveled limbs, but the young man who came toward her now was tall and lanky, and his suit hung off him because he was just a skinny kid. No more than nineteen. He carried a heavy suitcase in his right hand. It swayed back and forth like a leather guillotine.

As he approached the grandmother, the young man smiled: wide and white and toothy.

"Hello, ma'am!"

Surprising even herself, Alice welcomed him.

There were coffee cakes, Folger's Instant, some cookies

from a box. The young man declined politely. He sat down at the kitchen table.

"Tell me, ma'am, do you have an encyclopedia in the house?"

"We have a dictionary."

The young man smiled again and shook his head. He looked at the coffee cakes and then at Alice. "You know, ma'am, I think I will take a bite of that. If you please."

No more needed to be said. If Alice could feed this boy, if she could put some meat on those skinny bones, then all would be right. She cut him a slice and offered tea or pop this time, but he just said, "I'll have what you're having," and that meant two cups of Folger's, black.

"You know, a dictionary is a wonderful thing," he said after a small sip of coffee. "We have a whole line of dictionaries that put Webster's to shame. But a dictionary can only take you so far."

He paused for a moment, just long enough to conjure something in Alice she couldn't quite explain. What did this boy mean by saying a dictionary could only take her so far? So far to what? It was just a book with words and definitions. It pinned things down, solidified them. He talked as if a dictionary were a streetcar, but Alice knew it was nothing but a collection of ink and paper.

She looked at the clock. Joe would be coming in soon for his afternoon coffee. The boy would have to be gone by then, she knew. But why she knew it, she couldn't say.

"If you really want to make the home complete, ma'am, you're going to need an encyclopedia."

Her first thought was for the children. They could use it to write reports for school, help with homework. Might be good to have around. Of course, there were libraries for such things, but having an encyclopedia at home would make it more convenient. And yet, would the children even be here once school started?

The summer was still flush, and Annie hadn't said anything. Alice didn't know much about Annie and her movie-making, but she had a hard time imagining the job would take more than three months. Maybe it would. Annie was never one to plan ahead nor tell anyone her plans. Always flying by the seat of her pants and off in the clouds.

Alice sighed. She wondered how she'd failed so miserably with her own daughter. She and Joe had both worked so hard to instill responsibility, diligence, practicality. To have a daughter turn out so wayward was a bitter pill. Sarah would need to toughen up or she'd turn out like Annie, and then Alice would have two that she'd failed.

All the while, Alice never let herself think the other thought which haunted the back of her mind, the thought about Annie never coming back for the kids. That thought was too much to think about. Better to wonder if the kids would need an encyclopedia for school, if it came to that, and let the matter be settled.

"The first feature of our books, ma'am," the young man continued after he'd given the requisite time for his customer to dream, "are the brown leather covers. Supple and smooth, they make a handsome display on the bookshelf. Even if you never crack them open, you'll be glad of the purchase just for the beauty of that leather. Of course," he added quickly, "these covers are entirely ethical, made from the finest synthetics, polyurethane and polyvinyl chloride. No animals harmed. But guests and visitors will never know. All they'll see is the glorious sheen and elegance of the brown leather.

"Think of it this way," he was on a roll now, "these covers

are like the soft luxuriousness of leather interior in a Cadillac. I know we're here in Michigan, ma'am, home of the automobile, and I don't need to tell you how wonderful it is to sit back in a car with fine leather seating. Sit back in a car like that and you're ready to go places. Well, ma'am, it's just the same with an encyclopedia. Rub your hands over the cover of these books and get ready for an incredible ride."

Alice knew this was all a bunch of salesman patter, but she let herself listen just the same. The young man's eyes were so bright, so blue, framed as they were by his dark brown hair, that Alice didn't want to disappoint them. If she had been thinking more practically, she would have scolded herself for being so sentimental, but practicality had disappeared down her coffee cup, drowned in the Folger's.

"Shall we take a look, ma'am?" he asked, just a hint of a smile gliding across his lips.

Alice didn't see the harm. The young man was careful to wipe his hands so that no coffee cake crumbs tarnished those luxurious fake leather covers. Reaching down into his briefcase, the young man unzipped it slowly, and with much solemnity, he pulled out the sample.

Quickly, Alice moved the cakes and coffee tray to one side, giving the man room to lay his glorious wares. There upon the table, he placed the tome, heavy and thick as an old family bible.

"Now this is just the first volume, but let's take a look," he said, peeling the pages apart right down the middle, opening to an entry about architecture. "Notice the full-color pictures, ma'am. And the easy-to-read typeface. Cross-references at the bottom of each entry. Everything you need to make a world of discoveries. These books make it easy to find what you're looking for, and frankly, to find a few things you weren't looking for too."

Here he looked up from the page and tried to meet her eyes, his best-gleaming smile on his lips, but Alice was transfixed. She hadn't really heard a word he'd said. Instead, her eyes feasted on Versailles, and the flying buttresses of St. Paul's cathedral, and the gleaming gold rooms of the Romanov summer palace.

As a child, Alice had done well at school. She was diligent, careful in her work, and had the best penmanship of any in her class.

But those things she retained from her formal education had been only the practical things: arithmetic, spelling, the smattering of geography that mattered. She was sure she had studied Shakespeare, but to recite even a line of his verse was near impossible now. All those things—the histories and literature, the sciences and cultures—they had been lost not long after the diploma had been bestowed.

But when she looked at that entry for architecture, when she gazed at those marvels, she felt something she'd never felt in all her years of schooling

She had no word to describe it. It was a feeling beyond her many long years of marriage and childrearing, of working in her mother's grocery store, of the war and praying for Joe to return, of taking a job at the Falcon Show Bar so Joe could study for his GED, of late nights waiting for him to return from the swing shift, of mopping kitchen floors and making beds and cooking dinner. This feeling overwhelmed her. She couldn't name it or even acknowledge that it was real, but she felt it nevertheless.

Wonder. Awe. Longing.

"Well, ma'am," the man continued, trying to keep the spell

going even as he whispered his temptation, "what do you think?"

Alice mumbled something, though her eyes were still wandering the gardens at Versailles.

"Twenty-two volumes," the young man said softly. "Just think of that. Twenty-two volumes."

"Mmm," said Alice, her fingers now daring to turn the page.

"Go ahead, ma'am." The young man sat back in his chair and let her roam the landscape.

Alice was swept away to the mountains of Argentina, to the battlefields of Persia with Alexander the Great, to the Antarctic with Shackleton, across the whole vast realms of what could be contained in one letter of the alphabet, and as she explored, time melted away, the coffee grew cold, and a few stray houseflies began to find their way to the untouched coffee cake.

She never knew how thrilling reading could be, or if she had, she'd forgotten. This wasn't like reading a recipe in one of her cookbooks; it was like traveling to villages and cities and countries where such recipes were born. The photographs on each page leaped out at her, like she had stepped through a movie screen, and the stories in the words were more than knowledge; they were a new life that she had been reborn to live.

She didn't know how long she'd sat there reading the encyclopedia, but at some point, a throat cleared, and a hand with thin, strong fingers reached out and took the book from her.

"We only sell the best, ma'am," said the young man, locking the book away again within his massive briefcase. "That's just a sample, of course. If you want the full set, you'll have hours of reading ahead. There's no telling where you'll be swept off to."

Deftly, before Alice had quite come out of her daze, the young man pulled out an order form and a fountain pen. "Any children in the house?" he said, his words like the misdirection of a stage magician performing a trick. Before Alice realized what she was doing, she had taken the pen from him. "They'll have an essential tool at their fingertips with these books. Great for writing reports, studying for tests. The whole set, all twenty-two volumes, can be yours with our economical payment plan."

Now he was pointing at some figures on the form. Alice was nodding, eminently convinced of the practicality of such a purchase. She was signing her name, she was grabbing her purse from the credenza in the living room, she was writing a check with the first payment, she was casting furtive glances at the young man's briefcase in hopes that he might take out the sample book again, letting her wander once more through the vast territory of wonder and longing.

When he thanked her for everything, when he assured her of the wisdom of her purchase, when he stood up from the table and smiled and said he had to be going but that he'd enjoyed their visit, and my, what a gracious hostess she was, and he wished her good day, and God bless, and then he picked up his briefcase and took his brown suit out the door in long, lanky strides, Alice hardly knew what had happened.

A few moments later—not more than a few seconds—she looked for him out the window, but he was gone.

Impossible. The driveway was too long. *Where could he have gone?* Maybe he had a car parked by the side of the road. Alice convinced herself this is what happened.

That night, she dreamed of her father.

It was in the days before his cancer, when he used to sit in the sun outside the back door, polishing his glasses and chewing on tobacco, watching the field for stray cats and dragonflies. Alice would make glances at him as she played jacks in the dirt with her brothers, wondering what it was her father was doing.

He sat, legs outstretched, shoes off, and socks nestled in the brown, parched grass. Sometimes he would sit for hours, and all the while, whether she was out playing in the yard or helping her mother in the kitchen, Alice would wonder what her father meant by sitting there.

She wished he would do something, anything: play cards or whittle a stick or read a newspaper. Of course, he couldn't read a newspaper. Not in English anyway. He had never learned to read anything other than a smattering of Romanian when he was a boy in Braşov. To read now, to learn a new language, it would be too much.

But Alice wished he would do more than sit and stare.

When the cancer finally came, Alice remembered, her father never sat and watched the field. His sickness made him disappear.

The remainder of Alice's sleep was restless, though she couldn't remember any more of her dream. When the chores and duties of the next day came, she kept wondering why she never mentioned the encyclopedias to Joe.

And when a week went by, and she started looking out the window for the delivery truck, she noticed that Joe noticed her, but she still never said anything. He would find out eventually; when a heavy box with twenty-two volumes of books was dropped at their doorstep, he would find out. But for those few weeks, while she waited, Alice never told.

"The kids don't want these. They got their video games,

and Sarah's lost in all of Isabel's old books." Joe held up volume three of the encyclopedias—the gateway to Cleopatra and the California Gold Rush and Cadmium—and he shook his head derisively.

"For their homework, Joe," Alice replied. "Reports and projects."

Joe raised an eyebrow. He and Alice had not yet discussed what would happen when summer was over and their grandchildren still remained. The end of August was looming.

"Anyway," she continued, "they're good to have around. If we need to know something, we look it up. See?" She too picked up a volume and cracked it open. When the glossy pages peeled apart, that same wonder and longing she had felt weeks earlier flowed through her veins once more.

The spell was even stronger this time. The Cretaceous period loomed before her, filling her eyes with magnolia trees and volcanoes and dragonflies as large as a human hand, and herds of Parasaurolophus roaming the plains.

Alice sat down and started reading.

For the rest of the morning, Joe couldn't get a word out of his wife. She neglected the dishes, forgot about hanging the laundry, and left her tomato plants to wither in the dry heat.

Sarah watched her grandmother spend the whole day reading a book—thick and heavy, bound in leather like a magician's spell book—and when late afternoon came and the garden still needed watering, Sarah grabbed the watering can and did her best to soak the plants.

As she tipped the spout over tomatoes and basil and cucumbers, she stared back at the house, straining to see inside the large kitchen windows, to catch a glimpse of Grandma Alice and her book. Sarah didn't think it was possible that her grandmother could waste the day away reading.

But she wasted the evening too. Joe grumbled but warmed up leftover chicken, and Sarah and Jay ate cereal, and all the while, Alice read the encyclopedia. Where she wandered, her husband and the grandchildren never knew, but they watched as she drifted farther and farther away, through golden fields that only she could see.

At last, Alice looked up to see that darkness now filled the kitchen windows. Night had come and all the house was asleep. Dirty dishes soaked in cold suds; Alice could see them piled in the sink, but she didn't move from her chair.

She was still lost, wandering through the hills of Bohemia and the haunted streets of Prague. Her index finger kept her place on the entry for "Czechoslovakia." None of the domestic duties of the house seemed to matter to her. All that mattered was knowing more and traveling far, of searching the world for wonders.

She heard the stairs creak and then Joe's voice called. "Alice. Come to bed."

Just a few more pages. "In a minute, Joe."

A fear shivered through her. Fear of stopping, of closing the book, of leaving the landscapes of her imagination. Fear of dreaming, of being that little girl who wanders by empty fields and brown-suited vagabonds. Fear of what tomorrow might hold, of the spell breaking.

Joe was snoring again when Alice finally crept into bed. She lay awake for a long time, thinking of the next volume in the encyclopedia and what she would find there. She resolved to read again when the dawn came.

This whole business kept up for a week. Alice sat at the kitchen table and read her encyclopedias, Joe and the kids did their best to keep the house running, and Sarah kept an eye on her grandmother, wondering what had happened to cause such a change.

One morning, when Sarah had grabbed a volume to read, she saw an ordinary reference book, no different from the encyclopedias she could find in the library. There were no magic castles or dangerous sorceresses; no unicorns or quests to enchant the reader. What could possibly hold her grandmother's attention like this?

And yet, Alice Ray was enraptured. She read morning, noon, and night, only stopping to absentmindedly eat or use the bathroom, or when exhaustion came and she went to bed.

Joe was furious. He quietly seethed for the first few days, but by the end of the week, he was fed up. Hands on hips, he glared down at his wife, casting a shadow across the open book in front of her.

"Alice. It's gone too far. This has to stop. Either you do it, or I will."

She knew what he was asking of her. There was no other way. Things had gone off-kilter, the whole world had turned upside down. Somehow she had forgotten herself and what she was supposed to do and got lost in a dream. But the book lay open on the table, and the green vistas of Ireland were sprawled out before her, and she couldn't stop. She couldn't give it up.

"You'll have to do it, Joe. I'm not strong enough."

It only took a few minutes. The load was dumped in an old cardboard box, and the tractor drove it to the end of the long driveway, and a sign was propped against the mailbox: "Free Encyclopedias."

After a day, the cardboard box—loaded with treasure— was gone.

Joe was glad to see the dishes getting cleaned again, and laundry hung, and floors swept. Dinner and lunch and breakfast returned, warm and delicious. Sarah no longer watered the tomatoes.

And Alice felt like she had awoken from a foggy dream, the kind that comes during bouts of illness. It was good to get back to her duties.

But even as she returned to her chores and routines, Alice avoided the credenza in the living room. Without the encyclopedias to fill it, it felt empty. There were only the stray papers and old shoe boxes in the top drawers, and for several days, Alice avoided going into that part of the house. If she got too close, wistful feelings might return. So she kept her distance and tried to forget.

But after the fifth day, when the world, at last, began to take on its normal hue, Alice decided the credenza needed cleaning. Duster and polish in hand, she started wiping down the wood cabinets, lingering over the space where the books had been. When she came to the drawers, she lifted out the shoeboxes and set them on the carpet. She was almost finished when Sarah came up behind her.

"I'm surprised you're not running around fighting dragons," Alice said. "Or whatever you do in the woods." She bit her lip. The words tasted like acid on her tongue, and she regretted them instantly. Why did she say that to the child?

"Too hot," replied Sarah, who had developed calluses to her grandmother's put-downs. "What are these?" She had already opened one of the shoeboxes and found a pile of old photographs.

Alice's first instinct was to snatch the lid away and close the box, but she resisted. There was no harm in letting the child see. Just some old photos.

"That's me," Alice said, "as a little girl."

"Did you live on a farm?" asked Sarah, excitedly. The photograph showed a young Alice sitting atop a pony, two young boys flanking the beast on either side.

Alice laughed. "No, we lived in the city. That picture was taken at the circus. Though to call it a circus isn't fair, really. It was more of a traveling gypsy show. They had a few jugglers and acrobats, a fortune teller, and this pony you could ride for a nickel. Those are my brothers there."

More words tumbled out of Alice. She told Sarah about the fortune teller's tent, how she was afraid to go in, how her elder brother went onstage with the fire-eater, how the calliope man sang a song about Alice on the pony, and how the pony tried to nibble her dress.

"Who's this?" asked Sarah, reaching into the box and pulling out another picture.

The man's eyes stared into Alice's face, and she could see their piercing blue even though the picture was in black and white.

"That's my father."

"I thought you said you lived in the city. Why's he standing in a big field?"

Alice remembered. They lived on the outskirts of the city; their street ended where the field began, and in the hot summer, the field glowed a golden yellow. Her father used to walk the field sometimes, wandering after grasshoppers and dragonflies. His brown suit was one of the few things he owned when he crossed the Atlantic. Even on those hot days, he would wear it, like a skin he refused to shed.

The old woman took the photo from Sarah and placed it back in the box. She covered it with the lid and patted it gently as if the box were an old dog lying on the rug. Then she did her best to smile at the child.

"I know it's hot, but there's shade in the trees," she said. "Why don't you make up one of your adventures?"

"You want me to go?"

"No, that's not what I mean. I mean—" Alice broke off. She struggled to find the words. "I just want you to enjoy your days. Wander through those trees and do your daydreaming. Don't be stuck inside with me."

"But I liked hearing your stories and looking at those pictures. You never told me any of that before. It was like going back in time."

"Maybe I'll tell you more." Alice thought of all the things she could tell. Stories of the Depression and the war, of her father's stories and his boyhood in the old country, of meeting Joe and having babies. Of what it was like to lose her parents, to be orphaned.

She could tell Sarah more too. There were tales to be told of Versailles and Cleopatra and the volcanoes of Iceland: things that lived alongside her father in her memory, ghosts that walked right through her.

"When I'm done here," Alice added quickly. She picked up her duster again. "Go on now, go play."

Sarah got up slowly, her eyes stealing glances at the empty shelves. "Grandma," she began, "how come—?" But she never finished. Biting her lip and swallowing the words, she ran outside.

Alice was glad Sarah hadn't asked. After all, there was no good answer.

When she knew she was alone, Alice laid her hand atop the shelf and felt the smoothness of the finished wood. So empty. She wanted to be mad, but she wasn't. Disappointed, perhaps, but she knew it was for the best. A spell like that couldn't go on.

And yet there was a fullness inside her that was satisfying. She closed her eyes and saw herself standing in the golden field, watching the dragonflies and looking for stray cats.

Duster in hand, Alice got back to work.

CHAPTER SEVENTEEN
The Clay Mines

THEY HAD NOT GONE to the rusted gates since June, since
Sarah turned coward and refused to use the key.

But as July slipped through their hands like sand and
August crept over the forest like a blanket of marigolds, Sarah
knew they were running out of time.

She had crafted stories all summer: shooting layups alone,
sitting on her bed and staring at the covers of her paperback
books, fumbling through the contents of her secret shoebox,
fingering the Carolingian coins and twenty-sided dice. She
had skirted the edge of the forest too, since seeing the
creature on the Fourth of July, and kept mostly to the green
lawns and open spaces around her grandparents' house.

But there could be no more waiting, no more storytelling
in her head, no more excuses. She and Alex needed to run to
the gates and try to open them. The way to Avalon was real.
What else could the events of summer mean, except that there
was something in the forest which was tinged with magic?

Gates to Illvelion lay on the floor near her bed. Sarah hadn't
read it in over a week. The feeling that the book contained
some secret about the forest, about the gates, was too strong

and it started to disturb her. It was too real. She looked at the name of the author, emblazoned in yellow font across the front cover.

Who was this A.R. Rathmann? Sarah's imagination conjured outlandish scenarios.

He was a magician who had a crystal ball. He could see any corner of the world through its clear glass, and his eldritch vision led him to her forest and to the strange gates stuck in the middle of nowhere.

He was a time traveler. The gates had once belonged to a large estate, but all traces of it were now gone, and through his travels in time, he had witnessed the slow degradation of the property, until all that remained were the wrought iron gates and nothing else.

He was an eccentric, and it was he who built the gates as a joke, plopping them down in a forest clearing just for a laugh. He had done it elsewhere too, all over the country, dozens of gates to nowhere and attached to nothing. It was all absurd, and A.R. Rathmann laughed to himself whenever he thought of it. That's why he wrote his book, to have one more laugh at this immense, ridiculous joke.

Sarah let her mind wander through such flights of fancy, but each time she speculated about the author and his knowledge of secret gates, she couldn't shake the feeling that there was real magic at work, that something really did lie in the heart of the forest, and somehow A.R. Rathmann knew it. After all, hadn't she herself glimpsed the strange creature in the woods? Hadn't she seen something neither animal nor human stalking through the shadowed trees?

So the book sat next to her bed—unread for more than a week—while she tried to bury the eerie feeling it gave her and muster up the courage to visit the gates once more.

One morning, Jay was in a hurry. He barely chewed his sugar-puffed cereal.

"Where are you going?" Sarah asked, a bit annoyed. She didn't like when Jay's enthusiasm implied he had something adventurous to do. She wanted to be the one having adventures.

"Julian found it," her brother answered, mouth full of milk and cereal. "Clay mines."

"Clay mines?"

"That's what he called 'em."

Before she had time to think, Jay was dumping his half-eaten bowl by the kitchen sink and banging out the front door.

"Wait!" Sarah called, but her brother didn't notice.

Clay mines. Was that the same place as the clay-covered cliff she'd discovered in the eastern forest? Sarah felt defiant. She had found it, not Julian. He had come second, and he'd spoiled her solitude.

Sarah didn't even bother to eat breakfast. She raced out the door too, hoping to overtake Jay and the others and get to the cliff first.

But the eastern woods confounded her. After half an hour, she knew she was lost. Trying not to panic, she retraced her steps, all the while pushing toward what seemed like the direction of her grandparents' house. It felt as if the woods were trying to trick her. Every hint of a path or familiar tree turned out to be wrong. Every step pushed her further from where she wanted to go. Realizing defeat, Sarah knew she needed to stop searching for the clay mines and find some way out.

Another ten minutes later, she emerged from the woods into the backyard of Mr. Henderson. It was disorienting to end up so completely out of place, so far from where she had been aiming. But at least the long driveway was there, and Alex's house, and her grandfather's mailbox. Bitterness still swirled around her empty stomach when she thought of Jay and Julian and whoever else was with them, all having fun at the clay-covered cliff.

Still, she was glad to be out of the woods. That eastern side of the forest was all brambles and thickets, a kind of wilderness that frightened her. It was almost too wild, too untouched by human contact. And the way it seemed to change—how every twist of branch or vine was different depending on where she looked—made Sarah consider that perhaps magic had seeped into that side of the forest too.

Mr. Henderson's house was quiet and the window shades were drawn. His garden was a bit overgrown but verdant. Sarah wondered if he was on vacation. It was strange to think that someone would leave this place to go on vacation somewhere else.

For Sarah, this place—her grandparents' house—was a vacation, a getaway. Hidden between two patches of forest, silent and green and bursting with summer. Would it still be a vacation when fall came? Would she be here or in California again?

For a moment, her eyes drifted back to the eastern woods. They were thick with overgrowth. How could anyone find their way through it all?

Dejected, she loped back to her grandparents' house. When she got to the basketball court, she heard voices crackling from the garage. Jay and the others had returned, triumphant.

"A bowling ball?" Julian's voice snorted.

"It'll work, just wait," Jay answered.

"What's yours supposed to be, bro?" It was Jaime's voice.

"A naked lady. See the titties."

"Gross, dude!"

Sarah watched Jay come out of the garage, his hands coated in wet clay. He was shaking his head but smiling.

"Oh, hey," he said, nodding at Sarah. "I brought extra. If you wanna make something."

While Jay rinsed his hands with the garden hose, Sarah peaked into the open garage. Julian and Jaime were mucking about with slate-colored clay, making ill-formed sculptures and shapes. They had hauled the stuff from the cliff in a milk crate, and now it leaked mud and water all over Grandpa Ray's garage floor.

"I don't think they'll mind," said Jay, softly, as he came up behind his sister.

Sarah tried to pretend she wasn't hesitant or scared. Julian's eyes gleamed viciously, a tyrant in cargo shorts. Sarah didn't want to face his taunts or threats.

But then that defiance from earlier took over. "Why should *they* mind?" she hissed. "I'm the one who found that place."

Jay just shrugged. He didn't feel like figuring out Sarah's weird moods.

"Hey, nerd!" smiled Julian, catching sight of her and waving with mocking fingers. "Where's your little boyfriend? I couldn't find him this morning. He's due for his afternoon swirly."

"Shut up, Jules," said Jay, but there was no bite in his words.

"He's *your* brother," Sarah replied, trying her best to sound tough. "How should I know where he is?"

"Thought you two might be smooching in the woods,"

laughed Julian. "Anyway, I'm done here." He stood up and wiped the clay on his shorts. He and Jaime left their clay creations sitting on the garage floor. Jay reached down and picked up his lumpy bowling ball, moving it out into the sunshine.

"Good idea," Julian said, returning to his own sculpture and placing it in the sun. Once the boys had moved everything out to bake in the bright sun, they went down the driveway. Sarah was left alone with the carton of gloomy, watery clay. She peered over the edge to see how much remained, and for a split second, wondered if she should make something.

Now that she was alone, Sarah could let herself be jealous. But in her jealousy, she didn't want to give Julian or her brother any satisfaction. She would rather deny herself the fun of making something with the clay than let them know she envied their adventure.

"It's stupid, anyway," she told herself, even as her mind conjured ideas for what to sculpt. Something for Avalon, something for the real adventure she and Alex would have...

The sun was a tyrant. Heat poured over the grass and the pavement and the untouched waters of the pool, turning everything into fire. The clay sculptures hardened, their surfaces now brittle, their color like the dusty hide of an elephant.

Sarah left the heated world behind. She grabbed her wooden sword and shield from the breezeway and ran to the darkness of the woods: the western woods, where the creek flowed slowly toward the rusted gates, and where she hunted for wild blackberries.

But when she reached them, they were all dried up: leaves brittle, fruit devoured. All around her, Sarah felt the summer turn into kindling for the wicked sun. And soon, even the sun would give up, cool down its heat, and let autumn adopt the deadened world. Things were fading too quickly. She swung her sword at the thorny branches and refused to give in.

~

"SARAH!" Alex shouted from the edge of the forest. He was barreling down a steep hill toward her. Sarah was watching the minnows flit through the muddy creek, her feet dangling over the embankment. Alex had his sword and shield too.

Something was about to start. The summer wasn't going to fade just yet.

"Come on," said Sarah. She stood up and brandished her sword. "The queens have begun to chant their dark spells. If we don't hurry, the Oak-Hearted Knight will be destroyed."

They ran. Into the heart of the forest, their bruised knees and dirt-stained legs carried them, their blades of balsam wood at the ready. Sarah wasn't sure where they were headed. She only knew that she wanted to run, to be on a quest, to hurry into the hidden world of the forest.

Stories from all her books mingled together in her head —*Gates of Illvelion* most especially—and for a moment she hoped they might meet the strange creature who frightened her on the Fourth of July. She was ready this time, with her sword and her friend. She imagined a face on the creature, a face she would love to bash, a familiar face...

Alex had slowed his run. He looked warily at the trees as if searching for something.

"What is it?" Sarah asked.

Alex kept silent, but he couldn't stop looking for some sign of the sleeping knight. This part of the forest looked like the place where he had seen that strange vision.

"I think—"

"The queens?" said Sarah, her eyes shining. She loved it when Alex really imagined the game with her.

"Not really… Something else." Alex was distracted.

Sarah tried not to let it bother her. She was off into Avalon again.

"Do you hear it?" she said, grinning. "The first queen blows a silver horn. And the second queen sends up her falcon to call out an answer." Tilting her face up toward the sky, Sarah bathed in the blue and white and ever-encroaching grayness of storm clouds to the west. She could see the falcon soaring above the trees. "But then—"

She whirled on Alex and grabbed his wrist. "The third queen makes no sound as she creeps through the forest. Quick! Run!"

Then she was off again, sprinting deeper and deeper into the woods. She didn't even turn around to see if Alex was following. All she could do was hope.

The third queen followed, silent as an owl, gliding between oak trees in her pursuit. Sarah ran hard and swung her sword at imaginary bats. She danced and leaped over fallen logs; she was swifter than the silver unicorn.

At last, it was enough.

"I can't!" Sarah panted, out of breath, stitch in her side. She laughed as she stopped running and bent over to ease the cramp. She had come a long way, further into the forest than she realized. For a moment she feared Alex was gone, left behind, or returned to his house, but then his footsteps crunch through the brown leaves.

"Where are we?" he asked.

"Close to the third queen's cave. She doesn't want us to find her elixir of forgetfulness. We might use it to reverse the spell on the Oak-Hearted—"

"Do you know how to get back?"

Sarah could see the shadow in his eyes. They were black marbles, unwilling to accept the enchantment.

"I think. Maybe."

"Sarah, there's a storm coming."

"No, it's sunny."

It wasn't a convincing lie. Even Sarah didn't really believe it. The dark clouds from the west were moving closer.

"Just a bit longer," she pleaded. She was scared of the coming storm, but it frightened her even more that Alex seemed scared. "Look, over there."

The third queen's cave was a clearing in the woods, a little alcove where the brambles and young trees did not reach. Standing in the middle of it was an old porcelain toilet.

"What the..." Alex headed into the clearing, transfixed on the toilet. "Mr. Henderson was getting rid of this."

Sarah was just as confused. "Look at all this stuff."

There were a couple of old couch cushions turned into a makeshift bed, adult magazines strewn about in a pile, a faded orange water cooler that looked like it had been left behind from a softball game, and cigarette butts everywhere.

"I think we should leave," Sarah said. This time she was looking up at the sky. The dark clouds gathered. The sun was gone.

"How did..." Alex said to himself, inspecting the toilet as if the cracked porcelain would reveal a clue. Then he turned around and looked at the entire clearing. "Julian," he said softly.

"Let's go," Sarah pleaded. Thunder rumbled. Louder. Then again. "Come on!"

Alex didn't see it at first, but then he spotted a worn leather book shoved under one of the cushions. He pulled it out and flipped through it. Addresses, phone numbers, names of people he didn't recognize. It was their mom's address book, the one she used for work. On the last page were reminders of birthdays and anniversaries, a quickly scrawled note for Jaime's dentist appointment two years ago, and a man's name: *Rick.*

Below the name was a phone number, written in thick marker. Hasty but important. It was written across the other dates and names so that it dominated the page.

Questions raced through Alex's head. Why did Julian have this? Why did Alex feel a sinking feeling when he saw the name Rick and the telephone number? What was this place? How long had Julian been coming here? Did Mom even know her address book was missing?

But then, what could she do? She hadn't been around for weeks...

The storm broke. All at once, tiny droplets peppered the ground, pinging off the leaves and dirt like BB gun pellets. When they hit Alex and Sarah's skin, they exploded like firecrackers. Alex shoved the address book back under the cushion, then he and Sarah ran. Soaked with rain, they fled.

Soon the droplets grew into hard, heavy stones; water flooded everywhere. The forest floor became a swamp, and as the children ran, their footsteps left imprints in the muck. Mud slimed their shoes. Still, they ran, weighted with water, trying to outrun the thunder.

The wind bent the trees sideways. Lightning crackled not far away, striking a tree in the distance. Sarah felt panic rising up through her throat. The house was still too far. All she could think was the old warning: *Don't stand under a tree, don't stand under a tree, don't stand under a tree.* Trees were all around them. The forest was a trap.

They ran harder, and soon the muddy swaths of lawn opened before them. The forest expelled them. They dodged puddles like mine traps. The house was before them. Shelter. Safety.

They ran. Then they banged through the front door. They stood in the laundry room, dripping puddles on the linoleum floor, heaving for breath. When Grandma Ray saw them, she called them sad, wet puppies and demanded they grab some towels to dry off.

Then the tornado sirens wailed.

When they ran to the basement, Grandma Ray didn't bother to turn the lights on. The storm outside had blackened the sky, but still, Alice Ray didn't see the need. The glass door let in enough light.

The Ray house was built on top of a hill, and the hill sloped down in such a way that the basement was partly underground and partly open to the sloping hill. Joe had put in a glass sliding door so they could go in and out of the basement from outside, and he had paved a courtyard next to the door for the kids to play in. Annie had often used that door to sneak out at night and drink cheap wine with her friends on the courtyard pavement.

Sarah hated the basement. The only thing she had ever liked was the glass door, but right now, with the storm howling, she hated that too. She didn't want to stand near the glass, but going deeper into the basement was even worse. There was no escape. She moved as close to her grandmother as she could; it was the only place that felt halfway safe. The sirens wailed and the trees blew sideways.

It was a basement full of nooks and crannies, and Alex sought a corner to be alone in. Toward the back, there was a bamboo curtain cordoning off one section of the room. Painted on the bamboo was the image of a peacock in full plume. It looked like something out of an old kung-fu movie.

Alex lifted the curtain and it crinkled when he touched it, but he went underneath anyway, back to the secret space beyond. What he found was a hammock strung across the length of the area, hanging from rings bolted into the cinder block walls. He sat on the hammock, feet dangling down. The storm and sirens were distant sounds in his ears. Over and over he saw that address book flip its pages in his mind. Every time, they landed on one name. One word.

Rick.

He sat on the hammock and rocked and rocked and rocked.

The sky outside wasn't as dark anymore, but it wasn't bright either. It was pale yellow, almost white. Not the kind of light the sun would make, but a light that came from some hidden source.

"Is it over?" Sarah asked.

The trees weren't blowing anymore. Everything was still.

"Heard from Uncle John once that right before the tornado hit, it was like this. Everything stopped and then boom!" Grandpa Ray clapped his hands together and chuckled.

He had come downstairs earlier, just after the kids and Alice, but Sarah hadn't noticed till now. She squeezed in tighter to her grandmother.

"Joe," Alice scolded, pursing her lips.

"He was in a tornado, Alice," Grandpa Ray rejoined. "That's what he said."

"I think it's close to over," Alice said to her granddaughter. "The sirens have stopped."

"Where's the other one?" asked Grandpa Ray, looking around the basement.

"He's here," answered Grandma. "Behind the curtain. Or do you mean Jay? I think he's down with the Guerrera boys."

"Whichever one, I guess," said Joe, smiling. "Alex?" he called to the peacock curtain. "Careful you don't flip that thing!"

"Why do you have that down here?" Sarah asked her grandfather, tilting her head to the peacock. She hated how old and strange it looked in that cinder block basement, the way it hid that corner and made her fear what lay beyond.

"Brought it home from Okinawa. Thought it made a nice little decoration. Gives you some privacy."

"Your grandfather used to come down here and take naps," added Alice. "Why don't you anymore, Joe?"

"How do you know I don't?" Grandpa answered with a wink. "Anyway, I think the storm's over."

The sun was out as if there had never even been a storm. Everything was baking again in the crackling heat, only this time there was the added musk of rainwater and humidity in the air.

Sarah and Alex seemed to have forgotten their game. When they came back out of the house, puddles of water dotted the pavement around the sandbox and basketball court. The swimming pool looked like a good idea, although they'd have to skim out the leaves and twigs that had fallen in during the storm.

Just as Sarah rounded the corner to the changing shed, out

of the corner of her eye she caught sight of the garage, its door still open and the crate of muddy clay still on its threshold. Right in front of the door, were three globs of gray mud, each one dripping streams of clay and water into the pavement.

Sarah couldn't help but smile.

The fourth queen had worked her magic. She, the mistress of wind and rain, had stricken her foes' talismans into nothingness. No one but she would be sovereign of the eastern woods, and all who trespassed would know her fury.

"Hey, wait up!" Sarah called, shaking herself out of her daydream. She ran after Alex who was already in his swimsuit and onto the deck.

The sun blazed above them, an unflinching eye, watching the whole world burn. Summer would end in withering heat, in destruction, in storms that did not cool or quench.

But Sarah and Alex didn't care. They attacked the heat with two sharp splashes, breaking the surface of the blue water and extending summer for one more day.

CHAPTER EIGHTEEN

Oak Heart

Mrs. Fabrizio put the water on the stove to boil. She wasn't hungry, but she needed a cup of coffee. Troubling thoughts still drifted through her head since waking up.

Why had I dreamt that dream? she wondered. *How strange.*

She hadn't thought about France in a long time. Always fond memories, memories of Theo, but they were far from her mind these days. It didn't help to dwell too much on the past. She missed Theo deeply, but there was parish work to keep her busy, and those grandkids who thought they knew everything and played video games all day long. *That's what happens when the parents work all the time,* she thought.

Lina sighed. Her son's marriage was alright, and so was her daughter's, but her mind often drifted to them and their families and the kids who needed a good grandma to take care of them so they didn't forget what love was.

Why was she thinking about all of this now?

It was that dream. It had disturbed her sleep, scared her, made her wonder and now she couldn't shake the damn thing.

France. But it wasn't the France she and Theo had seen on their twenty-fifth wedding anniversary when he'd surprised her with the trip and they toured all the countryside and the cathedrals and vineyards. He had wanted to show her the beauty of this place once ravaged by war. A chance to reclaim the memories, he'd said. Make them happier. With her.

No, this France was different. Lina had been different.

A castle. Herself a lady in a wimple, waiting for her lover to return. But he never did. Day and night, season after season, she waited with her stitching and her weaving and her work in the house, and he never came. And she cried for him at night.

Then the dream changed and she was riding a horse, deep in the forest. Everyone spoke a strange sort of German. A hunting party of some kind, and she was the leader of it. It was one of those deep forests on the border between France and Germany.

She was still the lady, but this time with a hunting bow across her back and a small sword on her belt. She rode with the party for a time, but then she veered away, off on her own until she came to a small cave cut into the side of a hill.

A shrine. And here was her love, himself a hermit now, hair as white as a ghost, and he spoke to the birds and the sun as if they could understand him, and his wild eyes searched her face, but she wasn't sure he recognized her.

He wore a strange kind of breastplate, made of dried bark and fastened over his shoulders with ropes of twine. Smudged on the front with soot was the image of an oak tree, its branches in the shape of a heart. It was his only clothing.

Two coins for alms, she had said. *Two coins if you'll remember me in your prayers.*

He mumbled something to the dirt as his hands clenched the two coins. Then he began scratching for worms with a stick.

She had lost him, so she turned and rode away.

Then she woke up.

The pot on the stove whistled. Lina poured hot water into her cup; the freeze-dried crystals dissolved, and the bitter smell of coffee filled the little kitchen.

She knew what to do. After a stop at the pharmacy and the bank, Lina would go see the Rays. That was the answer.

"I LIKE how you two get out in the dirt and play," Mrs. Fabrizio said to Sarah and Alex. "You've got good summer faces, suntanned and smudged." She reached into her purse and pulled out two caramel candies. She dropped one each into the children's hands and then patted their heads. "Good kids."

Alice asked if Lina wanted to shuffle the cards.

"Not today, Alice dear," Mrs. Fabrizio replied. "I don't know if I have a head for cards. Bad sleep last night."

"Coming down with something?"

"No, I don't think so. Just tossed and turned. Restless." Lina laughed. "Theo would have nudged me and told me to stop squirming. Then he would've held my hand all night. Dear man."

Mrs. Fabrizio was lost in reverie for a moment. Alice shrugged and put down a plate of hard cookies to dunk in their coffee.

Sarah and Alex started to get up. They had adventures to go on, queens to fight, and secrets to uncover.

But Mrs. Fabrizio shook herself out of her memories and stopped them.

"A minute, dearies," she said. "Sarah, do you still have those old coins I gave you?"

"Yes," Sarah replied. "Sure. They're really great! I've been thinking about where they must have come from and we've sorta made them part of our game."

She looked sidelong at Alex, not wanting to say too much about what they'd been pretending. Then she looked at her grandmother, expecting some sort of disapproval.

But Alice was too busy looking through the sales catalogs that came in the mail.

"Cherries are a dollar and forty cents at IGC this week," Alice said to herself and no one in particular.

Sarah was hoping Mrs. Fabrizio wouldn't ask her to give the coins back.

"Would you mind getting them for a moment?" Mrs. Fabrizio smiled. "I have a sort of bet with myself and want to see if I'm right."

Sarah didn't understand what that meant, but she nodded. She pulled Alex's arm and the two of them rushed up to her room.

"She's probably gonna say they need to be in a museum or something," Alex said when they were alone in the bedroom. "Probably some lawyer said she had to get them back."

"No, she just wants to look at them," Sarah replied, uncertain. "That's what she said. Mrs. Fabrizio is nice. She wouldn't trick us."

"She wants them back."

Sarah didn't answer. She took out the shoebox that held all her treasures.

A few books from Aunt Isabel were there, with *Gates to Illvelion* buried at the bottom, and the twenty-sided dice, and the iron key, and jostled to the side were the two Carolingian coins.

"Lemme see 'em," said Alex, reaching into the box.

Sarah almost snatched the shoebox away, but Alex was too quick and she couldn't stop him. He held the coins up to the sunlight coming through the window.

"Cool! These are, like, a thousand years old?"

"More than that," said Sarah.

"You should tell her you can't find them. Tell her you lost them."

Sarah almost recoiled. She could never tell Mrs. Fabrizio a lie. The fact that Alex would suggest it made Sarah's face go red.

"No." She took the coins swiftly from his fingers, closed the shoebox lid, and went downstairs.

"She's gonna want them back!" Alex called out as he scrambled after her.

When Mrs. Fabrizio saw the coins again, she let out a little gasp.

"Clear as day," she murmured. "Same ones." She traced the faded relief on the coins with her index finger. For a long moment, Lina was lost in thought. She tried to hold on to the strange images from her dream.

"You can have them back if you want," Sarah said with a choked voice. She was so quiet that it seemed Mrs. Fabrizio couldn't hear her. "I bet they're valuable."

Lina felt the coolness of those coins and their rough, brittle edges and remembered how they felt in her dream, when they were new-minted silver and gleaming.

"Sarah, dear," Mrs. Fabrizio began, "may I tell you something? Alice, I'm going to take this dear girl for a walk. Come on, Sarah."

Grandma Ray mumbled something and kept looking at her sales catalogs. Alex stood by the kitchen table, unsure of what to do.

Sarah and Mrs. Fabrizio went out into the August afternoon.

"I dreamt about these coins last night," Mrs. Fabrizio said as they strolled to the back of the house. She still held the coins in her hand. "It was like I was in one of your King Arthur stories you play with your friend."

Sarah waited for Mrs. Fabrizio to say more, but the old woman was quiet. They were heading for the creek at the bottom of the valley, and when Sarah looked toward the edge of the woods on the far banks of the stream, she thought she saw something move between the trees.

"I don't know why," Mrs. Fabrizio continued at last, "but something about that dream keeps sticking with me. These coins..." She stopped and held them up in her palm. "These coins that Theo found. Why did I dream about them? And that strange man..."

"What strange man?" Sarah blurted out. She felt tingly all over. The movement in the woods had stopped. "I mean, I'm sorry I interrupted, Mrs. Fabrizio."

"Don't apologize, dear! I'm an old lady talking nonsense. Here," she handed Sarah the coins, "take them back. I just wanted to see if they were the same ones. That's all."

But something about the way Mrs. Fabrizio said it made Sarah think that wasn't all. There was a distance in Mrs. Fabrizio's eyes, a searching kind of look that made Sarah uncomfortable. She didn't like when older people seemed lost.

"They're part of your game now, isn't that so?" said the old woman after a moment. She still walked toward the creek and Sarah followed. "I like how you run around out here in the yard and the woods. Not glued to your video game screens."

"I'm not very good at video games."

"That's good, dear. Stay away from them."

Sarah wished she was better at video games. She wished Jay would invite her to play alongside him like he did with Julian and Jaime.

"Will you be staying on through the fall?" Mrs. Fabrizio asked, but then she bit her lip. She shouldn't have put the child on the spot. "Never mind. It's still summer, so let's think about that, shall we? No more talk of fall." She smiled at Sarah and wished she hadn't left her purse with the caramel candies back inside the house.

They came to the edge of the creek.

"Mrs. Fabrizio," Sarah began, "I've made these coins a special part of my game. There are these queens—more like witches, I guess—and they've captured this knight, and the only way to enter the kingdom is to pay the toll with these coins. They have this magical gate and nobody can enter without a key, and I added the stuff about the coins because I really liked them and thought it would be neat to use these real coins from so long ago, and I know you probably want them back and they should be in a museum or something and you had a dream about them and everything, but could you maybe wait until after I finish my game? I'll give them back after, I promise!"

The words came tumbling out of Sarah, but she couldn't help it. She felt guilty for keeping the coins from Mrs. Fabrizio, but they were wrapped up in her game now, and summer really was ending. Sarah was running out of time.

"Sarah, my dear," said Mrs. Fabrizio, reaching down to clutch the child's hand, squeezing it tight. "You can keep those coins forever. I don't want them back. It was just that dream, with that strange man who looked like my dear Theo, but wasn't. I just couldn't get those thoughts out of my head, and I decided if I could see those coins again, I might get some answers."

"Did you?"

Mrs. Fabrizio shook her head and laughed a little. "It was just a silly dream. Strange to see myself dressed up like a queen and that man with his oak tree shirt. Flights of fancy, that's all!"

But Sarah didn't laugh. "Oak tree shirt?" She shivered as she heard the trees rustling in the wind.

"Yes, isn't that funny? That's what I'd call it anyway. He had a piece of bark over his chest and it was painted with an oak with branches shaped like a heart. At least, I think it was a heart. I don't know where my brain conjured that from!"

"Mrs. Fabrizio," Sarah whispered, "that's part of my game. The Oak-Hearted Knight."

"Oh, well that explains it!" the old woman answered. "Heard you playing and it got stuck in my head without my knowing. Funny how the mind works!"

Sarah shivered again. She clutched the coins hard in her hands and watched the trees. There was no movement but the breeze, but in the darkness beyond the edge, Sarah strained to see if anything lurked there.

She was sure she had never mentioned the Oak-Hearted Knight around Mrs. Fabrizio. It was a secret part of her game, something that came from a wish she kept hidden in her heart. Only Alex knew. Mrs. Fabrizio had never heard of the Oak-Hearted Knight before.

"I like that name," Mrs. Fabrizio said. "Oak-Hearted. Almost like poetry." Mrs. Fabrizio looked at the trees along the creek bank. Their limbs and trunks cast shadows across the muddy creek water. "You are your mother's daughter," she continued. "Annie was just the same. Always coming up with stories and songs."

The woman smiled to herself. She never had much of an imagination. Life was just life. Good, bad, happy, or sad, it was enough to keep her occupied. Anthony and Kate, her children, were much the same. The simple act of living was enough for them.

But Lina had always admired the creative spirit in others. Theo and his paintings, all those farmhouses and vineyards he conjured out of his memories; she had loved them all, and she especially loved the look on Theo's face when he was in front of his canvas. A lost, dreamy sort of look, but flecked with intense passion. He was consumed in those moments, utterly possessed by the flames of his imagination.

Lina used to stand in the doorway of his studio and watch; Theo never said a word to her, but she didn't mind. To watch him paint with that look in his eyes was enough.

Doubt suddenly spilled through Lina like a toppled inkwell. What was she doubting? Her skin started to prickle, and she felt cold despite standing in the sun. It was like the shadows of the trees had crept past the creek and landed on her.

"What does it mean?" Lina said it under her breath.

Sarah shuffled uncomfortably. She wasn't sure she wanted Mrs. Fabrizio to know. "He's—" Sarah started. "He's supposed to be true to his lady."

Sarah didn't realize that Mrs. Fabrizio wasn't talking to her anymore. The old woman was speaking to ghosts.

"Oak trees are really sturdy," Sarah continued. "So, his

heart is like an oak tree. He won't give up till he finds his love in Avalon."

Oh, how Sarah wished it were real! To have someone so true, so faithful! If only such fidelity wasn't make-believe.

Lina didn't hear the girl, didn't see the sadness on her face. Lina was thinking about Theo and that lost look in *his* eyes, and his face was the same face as the man in her dream, the wild hermit in the cave.

She had lost him.

She had given him the two coins. All she could give. But he had knelt to scratch the dirt.

"Mrs. Fabrizio?" Sarah asked. "Can we go back now?"

∼

ALEX DIDN'T HANG AROUND. Mrs. Ray tried to convince him to eat something, but he shrugged her off. Sarah was still down by the creek, talking to that Mrs. Fabrizio.

Besides, he hadn't really felt like playing anyway.

Sarah's games were fun, but lately, Alex hated going into the woods. He worried that around every tree that wounded, sleeping man might be waiting.

He hadn't told Sarah about what he saw.

When he got home, the kitchen was dark except for the faint streaks of sunlight slipping through the window.

Julian didn't look up when Alex came in. He slurped cereal and stared at his guitar magazine.

Alex felt guilty watching his brother flip longingly through those pages. More and more Julian had been asking for an electric guitar, but their dad had refused.

The piano in the living room was visible from the doorway of the kitchen; its lid was closed and a thin coat of dust covered it. Alex knew his dad wanted to keep paying for lessons. Alex knew he should practice more.

But Julian's desire for a guitar was forbidden. That was not the kind of music Alejandro Guerrera wanted his sons to play.

"Where's Jaime?" Alex asked. He grabbed a bowl from the cupboard and poured himself some cereal too.

Julian shoveled in another mouthful. "I'm not his keeper," he said with a shrug. "I dunno. At Raul's probably. Fixin' cars or some shit."

Jaime had been spending a lot more time with those older guys. Raul and Lester and Scotty. High school seniors, they only showed up for shop class and the occasional dodgeball game in gym. Julian hated them. He couldn't even say why he hated them, except Jaime thought they were cool and Julian couldn't stand to be around them.

"Wanna play *Martial Kombat*?" Alex asked, feeling the tension every time Julian turned a page of the magazine.

"Suck dick, dorkwad," was Julian's reply. "I got better things to do."

"Just an idea," Alex mumbled. Ashamed, his face turned red.

Neither said anything for a while. The only sound was the crunch of the cereal.

Alex's face still burned hot. He watched Julian read his magazine and ignore him, and he felt powerless. He put his spoon down.

"So, did you call him?" he asked.

Julian looked up. "What?" He scowled in confusion.

"Did you call him?" Alex repeated. "Rick."

The spoon dropped, clanging against the bowl. Milk splattered on the table.

"What did you say?" Julian's teeth were gritted, his eyes narrowed like a viper.

"Rick. Did you call him? Is Mom… Is she there?"

"How the fuck do you know about Rick?" Julian's voice exploded off the walls.

Alex had never seen his brother so angry. Julian sat perfectly still, but anger burned in his eyes, a fathomless black flame of hate. He didn't move, but Alex could feel the heat of his brother's rage from across the table.

Slowly, Julian's seething anger shifted. Realization dawned. The address book, the clearing in the woods. His secret place.

"You're dead."

His voice was barely above a whisper. It was pure venom.

Alex knew he had less than a second to escape. He knew the beatdown that was coming.

In a blur, Julian lunged for him. The cereal bowls clattered to the floor, porcelain breaking, milk pooling across the linoleum.

Alex felt a thick hand grab his neck. Nails pressed into his skin, the air cut off from his windpipe. He was thrust back into the wall, shaking the picture frames above his head. All he saw were Julian's dark eyes, hating him.

Faint but unmistakable, the garage door chain sprang to life.

Both boys heard it, and for a split second, neither moved. Alex still struggled to breathe, Julian's hand still around his throat. They both knew what that garage door meant.

Dad.

Release, air, relief. Alex slumped to the floor. Julian was standing in the doorway now, the overturned chair and spilled milk between them.

"You're still dead."

Alex said nothing.

"Clean up this shit before he comes in."

Julian was gone. Alex could hear the side door to the garage open and then close. Scrambling, he grabbed a handful of paper towels and wiped up the milk. The broken bowls were tossed in the garbage. Just as his dad came into the kitchen, Alex had straightened up the chairs.

"Mijo," said Mr. Guerrera, "come help me carry in the groceries."

Without a word, Alex did as he was told.

CHAPTER NINETEEN

Sir Alex of the Toilet Bowl

WHEN THE TREE LIMB FELL, Sarah was in the kitchen. She heard the noise before she knew what had happened.

Grandma Ray was by the window and saw the whole thing. Like a giant's fist, the heavy limb of the oak tree crashed to the ground. Anyone who might have been under it would've been crushed to pieces. The trunk of the old oak was hollow inside where the limb had broken off. A shell of its former self.

"Thank God," Alice said under her breath. "Thank God you children weren't out there."

Sarah ran over to see what had happened. The splintered, shattered pieces of wood littered the ground at the edge of the forest. It had happened in an instant. The day was placid. Sun shining like any other August afternoon, not a cloud nor a breeze to disturb the day, and yet without warning and all of a sudden, the oak tree's heaviest limb had fallen.

Why? was all Sarah could think. *Why had the limb fallen? How could it have happened on a clear day like this?*

"Tree was dead inside," was all Grandma could say. She

was shaking a little as she put the last clean dishes on the rack to dry. "Thank God you kids weren't playing out there."

It would have been unlikely for Sarah and Alex to be playing in that exact spot when the limb fell, but still, Sarah knew what her grandmother meant. Anyone standing under that tree would've died for sure.

She hadn't been playing outside at all because she'd been waiting for Alex. He hadn't come over in three whole days, but still, she waited. As the days drifted closer and closer to summer's end, Sarah knew she was running out of time to go back to the gates.

But she didn't want to go alone.

Summer was almost gone, and the nine queens were ascendant. What if the fifth queen had made the limb fall? A warning.

Sarah ran up to her bedroom. Jay was gone, maybe riding his bike, maybe playing video games downstairs, leaving Sarah alone to look at her treasures. She lifted the tattered lid of the shoebox and pulled out the iron key and the two coins. *Gates to Illvelion* flashed its golden cover at her, but she wasn't quite ready for it yet. She didn't want to finish the book until she had finished her own quest.

The bike pedals chugged along, the house and the expansive yard drifted away behind her, and Sarah headed down to Alex's house. No more waiting. She would go to him.

When she got to the house, the windows were dark. No lights on. No sounds. She knocked at the back door and waited.

Nothing.

She tried the front door, and still no answer.

"They're out," came Mr. Henderson's voice. He was hauling boxes to the side of the road. "Left this morning."

"Oh," was the only thing Sarah could say. She watched the old man set boxes on the curb, some of them overflowing with pottery and picture frames. It looked like Mr. Henderson was getting rid of his old artifacts. Sarah fought the temptation to go look through the stuff. She was afraid of Henderson and what he might say.

There was nothing left to do but leave. Sarah rode her bike back down the driveway, but just as she passed the big tree in Alex's backyard, she saw the path leading from his lawn into the woods. She swerved her handlebars and headed through the tunnel of trees.

This was the young wood, with thin trees and light filtering down in wide beams, illuminating the puddles of green leaves that coated the ground.

Where was Alex? When would he be home?

Sarah felt herself growing anxious by the moment. The path was barely a path, all knotted roots and rocks beneath her tires. With each bump, her bike slowed until it was a struggle just to pedal. Sarah pushed harder, straining her calves to keep moving.

She knew the way back to her grandparents' was westward, but without a clear path, she couldn't be sure which direction she was going. The trees were thicker here, and the sun fought to break through the heavy foliage.

Sarah's neck prickled with sweat and creeping fear. Something else was in the woods. She just knew it. But everywhere she looked was only tree and shadow.

There!

Striding like two walking sticks, sending birds fluttering into the air.

But no. It was just a branch waving in the breeze.

Or there!

Head turned to watch her, two dark eyes unblinking.

No. A hollowed-out hornets' nest, its gray cone punctured by two small holes.

Sarah pedaled faster, harder. These were just tricks of the imagination. Only tricks.

The creature. A fairy or a ghost or a warrior sent by the queens. Made of bone or starlight or mounds of dirt, it was stalking her, always hidden beyond the corner of her eye.

Grandpa Ray's green lawn came into view. An exit from the forest. Sarah pushed, her legs burning.

When she wheeled out of the woods, she sped up. Her tires hit the lawn. Splinters of oak wood flew in all directions as the bike plowed through the debris.

The broken limb.

Sarah turned the handlebars. She swerved toward the house, toward the pavement, toward the swing set and the basketball court and the pool and all the ordinary things of summer. She almost swerved into Grandma Ray, hanging up laundry on the line.

"Come get your lunch," Grandma said.

Sarah ate lunch and kept looking out the window. Nothing outside but sunshine and heat.

Reruns on the television. Reading in her bedroom. Rolling the twenty-sided dice just to keep her hands occupied. Sarah was bored, but that's not what kept her inside. It was that feeling—that prickling on her neck in the forest—that told her something was waiting for her.

No one would believe her, but she knew it was real.

Sarah stared at the slanted ceiling of her bedroom. In a few week's time, she'd be eleven. And the new school year was waiting just beyond the edge of her eleven.

Sixth grade.

No more kids' stuff, elementary school, recess, playtime. Sixth grade. Bells ringing to change classes every fifty-five minutes, teenagers in the hallway towering over the younger kids, lockers and schedules, and if Jay was right, no more time for make-believe or adventures or fairy tales.

Sarah didn't want summer to end. No kid ever does, but this summer especially. Where would she be in four weeks? Which hallway would she trudge down? What would she do with all her stories, with the nine queens and the gates and Avalon? Would she feel the California sun or the Michigan one?

Late afternoon came at last. Sarah couldn't keep herself inside anymore. She played a game on the lawn, swinging her balsam sword at the air. The queens had surrounded her, their magic swirling in gusts like dandelion seeds caught on the wind. She held her shield firm. The coat of arms was that of a unicorn: horn the color of sea foam, mane like golden waves. It was only a child's painting, but to Sarah, it was as noble as the great unicorn Gallien himself.

The queens were closing in, and Sarah alone stood between them and the Oak-Hearted Knight.

"You shall not have him!" she cried.

She didn't expect a response, but from far off down the driveway came a voice, clamorous and sharp.

An enemy.

"Hear ye, hear ye!" the voice cried out in mockery. "All hail the great hero!"

Sarah froze. She watched as Julian sauntered down the pavement, pulling someone behind him. The other boy hung his head low as Julian dragged him by the white porcelain ring around his neck.

A toilet seat.

Julian held a circular piece of plywood under his other arm, the same hand clutching balsam wood. He pulled the boy along like a horse in harness.

"Come and see the great knight, Sir Alex of the Toilet Bowl!" Julian cried, cackling at his own prank. "The mightiest plunger of wicked turds! The savior of the shit stain! The valiant defender of defenseless piss!"

Julian threw him toward the grass in front of Sarah. Alex stumbled and fell to his knees. He kept his head low, the toilet seat weighing him down. Julian stood over him, raising the sword and shield high in the air.

"Here is your mighty blade!" Julian cried. The balsam wood splintered and broke as he cracked it across his leg. He tossed the pieces to Alex like scraps to a dog.

"And your shield!" He flung it like a frisbee toward the edge of the forest. Then he kicked Alex in the side, knocking him flat on the grass.

"Stop it!" Sarah cried. She rushed at Julian, slamming into him with her own shield. He laughed as she bounced off, a gnat against a storm.

"You want some too?" Julian said, reaching for Sarah's sword.

She stumbled away, pulling her sword back just in time. "No! Stop!" she yelled.

Tears came down now while Alex just lay in a heap beside her. Sarah's face was hot and her chest tight. Julian's sneering laugh, his lanky body standing there so relaxed and unaffected made her stomach roil. She wanted to hurt him. She wanted to stop him. But she wasn't strong enough.

"That's for messing with my shit," Julian said, leaning over Alex and spitting on him. "Have fun, losers!" he called out over his shoulder, laughing as he went back down the driveway.

Sarah dropped her sword and shield and stared at Alex. He still hadn't moved.

"Alex?" Her throat felt so dry. "We can make another sword. I promise."

The sun was getting lower in the sky. There was still time to make it to the gates, but the day was fading quickly. They could always go tomorrow, or another day, but Sarah felt a painful urgency that it had to be *right now*.

"Alex?" She knelt.

He was shaking, sniffling hard to hold back the tears.

"It's okay," Sarah said.

"No, it's not!" His voice sounded like Julian's. All venom.

When Sarah reached out to help him stand, he swatted her hand away. "Leave me alone!" He scrambled up from the grass, took the toilet seat from around his neck, and flung it in the same direction as his shield. "This is all your fault!" He was crying now, he couldn't hold it back. His dark irises were surrounded by streaks of flaming red; the skin around his eyes swelled.

"My fault?"

The sixth queen was triumphant. Her bewitching spells had ensnared Alex. He was under her thrall, speaking lies and believing falsehoods.

"Your fault," Alex said, darkly. "Making me play with you. Those stupid games. Running around like idiots with those dumb swords and all your fairy-tale baby stuff. I'm sick of it. I've had enough."

"I didn't make you play with me!" Sarah's own anger started to rise. "You wanted to play!"

"I didn't!"

"You had fun!"

"I was just bored," he said, looking away from her. "Nothing better to do. That's all."

"But—" Sarah's eyes stung. All the words inside her mouth had been crushed.

"Sorry," Alex said, his eyes still looking elsewhere. "I gotta go."

"What about the gates?" Sarah said, desperation setting in. "I'm ready now! I have the key!"

"The gates aren't real, Sarah. There's no magic. Nothing on the other side. Just stop pretending, okay?"

Sarah couldn't answer. A chasm had opened between them deeper than the earth. His face pitied her. She was a child who needed to learn that tooth fairies and Santa Claus and birthday wishes weren't real.

Alex turned to go, ambling back down the driveway, leaving her world forever. "Maybe we'll see each other at school," he said, trying to smile, trying to pretend that none of what just happened mattered. "If you're still here."

Sarah didn't see him. She barely heard him. She stood completely still, staring at the treetops as a breeze shook their boughs. The leaves of the quaking aspens carried a message from deep within, calling out to Sarah from that hidden kingdom.

Her fingers felt inside her pocket.

The key.

It was cold to the touch.

Bending down slowly and without a word, Sarah picked up her shield. She picked up her sword. She never looked back at Alex. She ran toward the woods.

~

HE'S WRONG, she told herself. *I'll prove it.*

Across a sea of leaves, all browns and rust-colored reds, and branches and wet earth and toadstools growing along sodden, hollowed tree trunks. The forest was a blur, a mixture of trees and hot tears, but Sarah knew exactly where she was going. Up ahead was the bridge.

Sunlight slanted down through the trees like a golden waterfall, casting a glow across the fallen oak. Sarah held her breath. A deep muddy brown with no bottom in sight, the waters of the creek below swelled and rushed underneath. They seemed higher than she remembered, rolling faster like a torrent.

If she fell… who would hear her fall?

One step—a sneaker toe on the slick bark—and then another, and there was no turning back. Sarah's hand was so sweaty, she worried she'd drop her sword. Her shield was a heavy weight on her arm, tipping her sideways. She tried to compensate, to shift her weight to the other side, but she went too far. She wobbled. The waters foamed and slushed under her. She was going to fall, or else her sword, or she would freeze and never move again.

The seventh queen had trapped her. The world around her blazed like a conflagration of sunset fire. She couldn't go move forward; she couldn't go back. She was suspended above the waters, a tightrope walker who had finally lost her nerve.

The balsam wood sword sank into the muddy stream, then bobbed up to the surface and floated away, another twig emptying into the Rouge River. But it became greater now than it had ever been before: a sword lost on a desperate quest. A sacrifice.

Sarah let her shield slip off too. It slammed into the water but didn't sink. It hit the surface and fought back, churning through the currents in search of the sword. The face of the unicorn gone, sunk below the unceasing current.

Unburdened, Sarah found her footing again. She did not wait. She did not glance at the muddy creek and the treasures flowing past but kept her eyes fixed upon the way forward, upon the edge of the bank and the path to Avalon.

She ran when her foot hit solid earth. She didn't wait to see if the bees would find her. Up the sloping hill, through the ever-darkening thicket of trees, until her feet carried her to the clearing.

It was dusk. The sun and the moon hung in the sky together, one at her back—a disk as orange as flame—the other a shimmer of translucent gray cutting a hole in the dark sky above her. The clearing seemed older now: more tall grasses, and wildflowers starting to turn brown, and grasshoppers and dragonflies marking their territory, flitting and flying across the golden meadow.

And the gates. They had not changed. They stood as solemn and inexplicable as ever.

She had to fight against Alex's words, against his doubts. These gates were special. They were the guardians of something. It wasn't a game. There was magic here.

She felt the key in her pocket, the surface of the iron a little rough against her fingers. She had forgotten the coins, the payment to the queens. Sarah felt her aloneness like a stab to the gut. No one knew she was here, no one knew this place except Alex, and he was gone. Who would find her if she became lost? Would the eighth queen, the guardian of the gates, let her escape without payment?

A rustle of leaves startled her.

I am alone, she told herself. *There's no one else here.*

But there had been a noise. The crunch of something underfoot. Sarah had no sword, no shield. She looked around the clearing, her heart racing.

The faerie knight? The creature? The eighth queen?

The grasshoppers paid her no mind. Like brittle leaves springing to life, they leaped from the tips of pitcher thistles like skipping stones. Sarah wanted to like them, but when they buzzed too close she shivered.

I must go. If I stay here, I'll forget. I'll grow old like all the rest...

She took the key out of her pocket, her fingers holding it tightly. Her palms were sweaty; she worried she'd drop it.

The gates waited there, indifferent to her quest.

When she stood close to them, her body inches from the wrought iron frame, Alex's voice came unbidden again.

Just stop pretending, okay?

Doubts seeped through the spires of the gates... just someone's property that never got finished, a house that once stood but now was torn down, nothing special, nothing on the other side... Just an ordinary thing left undone.

The sun was sinking fast. Soon it would be twilight and the way back turned to darkness.

Sarah put the key into the lock. Her hand trembled as she tried to turn it. She wasn't sure if it would turn, but she had to try. She wasn't ready to let go.

There were no coins to pay the eighth queen, no sword to fight the creature, no shield to protect her from monsters.

Only Sarah.

The key turned, and the gates unlocked. Sarah pushed her hands on the iron spires and the gates swung open.

Nothing was different on the other side. The same clearing beyond as behind.

But Sarah knew better. She knew what waited for her. She left Alex and Julian and all the voices of doubt to the whispering grass and stepped through the gates.

Into Avalon.

CHAPTER TWENTY
The Ninth Queen

THE FLAT GROUND BECAME A HILL. Up a steep incline, where the trees thinned out and became saplings, Sarah trudged, unable to see beyond the edge of the hill.

There was no eighth queen. No one had barred her way. The sunlight was stronger here, past the dense forest, up on higher ground. Maybe the eighth queen only came out when the sun wasn't in its last gasps of day. Maybe Sarah carried too much desire with her. The eighth queen didn't dare stand against such longing.

The hill crested and Sarah held her breath. What wonders would she find? Would it be like Illvelion, a castle of stone and mist waiting beyond? Or one of her other books? Or her own stories? Did the Oak-Hearted Knight wait for her, the final queen holding him in her charm?

Her sneakers mashed down the grass, staining their white soles. Her heart raced. The back of her neck was sticky from sweat; her hair clung to her skin. She came to the top of the hill.

The woman was kneeling, digging out weeds from her garden. She didn't see Sarah come over the hill.

A backyard. A house. A driveway that led to a subdivision beyond. This was Avalon.

"Oh!" The woman saw Sarah now. She was startled seeing the child there, all sweaty and dirty-kneed, standing at the edge of her property.

Sarah stood frozen. She was trespassing.

"Hello," the woman said, putting down her trowel. She stood up and took off her gardening gloves, then she wiped her forehead and took off her wide-brimmed sunhat. Sarah could see that she was elderly, with sagging cheeks and a shock of white hair cropped close to her scalp. Her eyes were large and piercing, like an owl's, but pale blue and watery around the edges. She was incredibly tall. Much taller than even Grandpa Ray. "Can I help you?" she asked.

Sarah had no voice. She had used up all her courage to open the gates.

"I won't bite, I promise."

Sarah didn't know what to do. She had no answer for why she was there.

"Did you come out of the forest? All by yourself?"

"I—" What could she say to this woman? She was a fool to think there was magic here.

"I'll start," the woman said, smiling. She held out a hand. "I'm Agnes."

"I'm—" Sarah tried to move. Was this all there was? A house and a garden and an old woman? "I'm Sarah." She stepped forward and shook the woman's hand.

It was a firm hand, much bigger than Sarah expected. Powerful. Strong. Sarah felt small and fragile as a bird's wing inside that grip.

"Now that we've established names, why don't you tell me

what you're doing here? Exploring? It's getting late, you know."

The sun was dipping lower. The sky was clear and the moon was bright in the eastern sky. Sarah realized that she would have to go back through the forest in twilight. Was this when the creature would find her?

But then, there was no creature. There was no Avalon either. No queens, no knight, no magic. This wasn't one of her books where the heroine found a portal to Faerie. This was just an ordinary backyard.

All those things she'd seen... thought she'd seen... Misplaced hopes...

"Listen, Sarah, the mosquitoes have decided they want to eat me for dinner. Why don't you come in and have a glass of lemonade and maybe give someone a call to pick you up? I don't like the idea of you going through those woods after sunset." Agnes picked up her trowel and started toward the house.

Sarah wanted to run, but she didn't want to run either. Where would she go? Back to the forest? Into the dark?

She followed.

Agnes's house was older than the others in the subdivision. A bungalow built around the same time as her grandparents' home, it was small but not cramped. The back door led right into the kitchen. It hadn't been refurbished in ages, but everything was clean. The countertops were clear of clutter, and the little Formica breakfast table was bare except for one small glass vase and a gathering of snapdragons inside it.

Sarah caught a peak at the next room, the living room, where bookshelves lined the walls in every direction. She strained to see what kind of books they held, whether they were just for show, or something more...

"Don't be shy," Agnes said. "Have a seat." She took down two large glasses and pulled a pitcher of lemonade out of the refrigerator.

From Sarah's seat at the table, she couldn't see the bookshelves anymore. She wanted to crane her neck to see around the corner, but she didn't want to be rude.

Agnes saw Sarah's eyes glancing sidelong. "We can sit in there if you want," she said. "Just use a coaster on the coffee table." She winked at the child, then finished filling the glasses. When Sarah hesitated, Agnes nodded her head toward the doorway. "Go on. It's just a house. The rooms enjoy it when we go in them."

Sarah walked through the open doorway into the living room. The room was dim and laden with heavy furnishings: dark wooden floors and dark wooden bookshelves, a sofa of rich burgundy upholstery, and an intricately woven rug in the center of the room that looked like it came from Mr. Henderson's collection of artifacts.

And books. Books everywhere. So many books that the shelves couldn't hold them all. Books spilled onto the floor, and nestled atop other books in rows on the shelves, and lay in stacks on the end tables. Books upon books upon books.

Sarah wandered along the edges of the room, scanning every title, every word.

These were not for show. History and philosophy, and books about archeology and religion, and books written in French and Persian, and folklore and mythology, and novels and novels and novels, old and new, hardcover and paperback, all of them with names that promised adventure or mystery or monsters or new worlds. Jeweled covers that reminded Sarah of the Science Fiction and Fantasy section at the Book Depot. Dusty paperbacks with titles like *The*

Waking Gryphon and *Stormworld* and *Zazamaz the Arcane* and...

Gates to Illvelion.

Sarah stopped. Her blood froze. This book. Here. In the house past the gates. This book that seemed to know every footfall of the forest and promised magic under its boughs.

Gates to Illvelion by A.R. Rathmann.

"Found them, eh?" Agnes said, carrying in the drinks. "There's more on the other shelf too. Over there." She nodded to another shelf stuffed with old paperbacks. "Should have pegged you straight away as the type. Sprang like a frightened rabbit out of the forest, after all. What could be more fantastical than a girl who shows up at dusk from beyond the gates?"

Beyond the gates?

Sarah turned half expecting Agnes to be transformed. Into what, she wasn't sure, whether witch or creature or fairy or something undreamed of, but something strange nevertheless. And here was Sarah, standing in her house waiting to be trapped.

Agnes had set the lemonades down on the coffee table. Then she sat down herself, her long legs pulled in tight to fit between the sofa and the table. She seemed almost too big for such a small space.

"Honestly, I don't recommend those," Agnes said, pointing with a long finger to the books directly behind Sarah. "Try some Silverfish or Juan Phillips Armstrong. Phil was always great fun at parties."

Sarah turned back to the shelf. She looked again at the yellow lettering of *Gates to Illvelion*, then her eyes wandered to the books beside it... *Hobart's Gambit*, *The Bone Breakers*, *Calliope's Magic Coat*... all by the same...

"A.R. Rathmann," Sarah said under her breath.

"Yes?"

Sarah wanted to reach out and pull down one of the books. What wonders did they promise? Were they like *Gates to Illvelion*, or was it that book alone which contained all the magic?

"Listen," Agnes continued, as matter-of-fact as Grandma Ray talking about coupons, "you're better off with something else. Feel free to borrow any other books. I don't mind. Have you read any Patchett?"

"I've read this book," Sarah whispered, pulling *Gates to Illvelion* off the shelf.

Agnes scoffed, waving a hand at an imaginary odor. "Rotten stuff. My apologies."

"I don't think it's rotten."

"I forgot," Agnes replied. "Kids don't know when something's crap."

Sarah pointed to the back of the book, her passion roused. "But look what it says. 'One of the best of all time!'"

"I don't control what the publisher slaps on there."

"But the bookseller? The man who gave it to me said it was the greatest fantasy he'd ever read."

"It's out of print. Hard to find. People get these notions that if something's rare it must be valuable. I'm sure there are fools out there who think that book is good simply because they've been told it's good by other fools."

Sarah was silent for a long time. She fought back tears that had come without warning. "Well," she said, her voice strained from holding herself together, "I still like it." She wasn't going to let this old spider in her burgundy web make her doubt.

"Children like everything. They don't yet know how to discern."

The tears did come, a little. Sarah couldn't help it. "Why do you have it, then? If it's so terrible?"

"My daughter made me keep it. Just like you, she thought it was worth something. She made me keep all my books." Agnes pointed again at the books behind Sarah. "I'd just as soon have them pulped, but I'm too lazy, I guess. So there they sit, taunting me every step of the way. Reminding me of a failed career…"

The bitterness in the old woman's voice jarred something in Sarah. She swallowed a sob and steadied herself. "Career?"

"Not much of one. Those five books and an unfinished manuscript that haunts me to this very day. You know what one newspaper wag dubbed me after my debut novel? 'An inscrutably brilliant enigma.' How can someone live up to that bullshit? I was paralyzed for years. Managed to eke out a couple more books then started to hate the whole damn thing. All of it." Agnes took a long, slow sip of her lemonade, leaving a red lipstick stain on the glass's rim.

"You…" Sarah was trying to make sense of it all. "You wrote this?" She almost dropped the book in her hand. It felt slippery all of a sudden.

Agnes rubbed the lipstick stain with her long thumb and stared into the glass like she was reading tea leaves or looking for a lost earring. "I sat at a typewriter and plunked out some words. Call that writing if you want. I never managed to get the hang of it. Disappointed myself every time."

Sarah stared down at the cover of the book.

A.R. Rathmann.

She had imagined a million different faces, a million different mysteries, all of them strange and wonderful and shrouded in secrecy. All of them *A.R. Rathmann*, the fantasy author who must have discovered the secrets of the gates and knew the magic of the forest.

What she had never imagined was an A.R. Rathmann who lived in a subdivision and gardened like her grandmother. A saggy-cheeked old lady who seemed to hate everything she'd ever written. A bitter woman without any hope.

"Are you really...?" Sarah began, unable to put her surprise, and disappointment, and disbelief into words.

"If you're writing sword and sorcery, all that pulp fantasy stuff," the woman replied, "you can't publish under a name like Agnes Smith. Nobody buys a book from an Agnes. My agent suggested the 'R' because he thought it sounded more sophisticated. 'Rathmann' was the name of a butcher who used to have a store over on Eight Mile and Lahser back in the fifties. Put it together, you get 'A.R. Rathmann.'"

The gates had led her here, to the living room of the author whose book had captivated her all summer.

"Listen," Agnes continued, "I shouldn't be so mean. You like the book. Okay, good. You go on liking it. Who am I to judge? Like the things you like, Sarah, and don't let anyone tell you differently."

Sarah had too many questions. They were all a jumble of thoughts bouncing around her head. She wanted to look at the other A.R. Rathmann novels, to ask Agnes about her career, to tell her the stories she'd been making up, about the nine queens, and Avalon...

"The gates," Sarah said at last. "You saw them too."

Agnes tilted her head, eyes smiling. "I used to take long walks in those woods. Long walks are great for ideas. Going through those gates felt like I was stepping into another world. They were so strange just sitting there, not part of anything, just abandoned. I can see you felt it too."

Sarah nodded.

"I wish my story had lived up to those gates. To all the things I thought I saw in that forest. I wish I had been able to make them real. For your sake. And mine."

"I—" Sarah felt her skin tingle. That same feeling from before, where she thought she saw something out of the corner of her eye.

She thought of all her adventures, of all the stories she had tried to conjure that summer. Of all the things she'd wished for and wanted to happen.

"I haven't finished it yet," Sarah confessed. "The book. I'm almost done, but…"

Agnes stood up and pulled open a drawer in one of the end tables. She took out a pen. "Want to make that bookseller's head explode? Show him this next time you stop in." She took the book from Sarah's hand and signed it. Then she handed it back.

"I already have a copy," Sarah said.

"I know. Have this one too."

WHEN GRANDMA RAY came to pick her up, it was near dark. The two elderly women exchanged pleasantries, and Alice Ray apologized for Sarah's intrusion.

Agnes Smith said, "No trouble at all," and gave Sarah a wink.

After the drive home, Sarah ran to her room faster than the bats flitting across the darkened lawn. She barely said hello to Grandpa Ray who sat on the couch eating his popcorn. Jay was in the spare room playing video games.

Flopping onto her bed, Sarah wasted no time. She flipped

through the pages of her book until she found the last chapter. As she started to read, she remembered the inscription Agnes had written inside the front cover:

"For Sarah, who came through the gates and softened the heart of the queen. May you someday write a better book than this one! Much love, A.R. Rathmann."

CHAPTER TWENTY-ONE

Sonata

"Is this Rick?"

"Yes."

The car traffic on the road had suddenly gotten louder. Julian could barely hold the plastic receiver in his hand, his palm was sweating so much.

"How can I help you?"

Rick's voice wasn't what Julian expected. It was pinched and nasally. Weak.

A million words went through Julian's head, but he didn't say any of them. He hung up.

Shoving his hands into his pockets, he slouched his way from the pay phone to the pizza place at the corner of the strip mall. He felt around for a few spare bucks crumpled in the crease of his left pocket.

He ordered a single slice and ate it on the curb, alone.

"Screw you, Rick," he said between bites. He had the courage now.

"Hey, no loitering!" A pot-bellied manager from the drugstore two doors down grabbed a stray shopping cart from the parking lot and frowned at Julian. "Come on, kid. Beat it."

Wiping the grease on his jeans, Julian stood up and hopped on his bike. The pay phone glared at him like a robotic cyclops, its gaping rectangular eye staring him down and daring him to call Rick back.

What for? Julian thought. *He's not gonna tell me.*

The houses rolled past him as he pedaled home, each lawn mowed and manicured, each porch draped with flower pots and welcome signs, each driveway just perfect for two perfect cars and two perfect parents.

"Go to hell," Julian wanted to say to every one of those houses. But he didn't. What good would it do?

The metronome was clicking like a bomb when he got home. Alex's fingers were gliding over the piano keys, making lilting melodies.

Julian slammed his bedroom door and tried to drown out the music. He fell on his bed and didn't bother to move the magazines that littered the mattress. They crinkled under his weight and stuck to his bare arms.

Alex always got what he wanted. Piano lessons, a new backpack, that latest Game Bot game. Julian got shit. A hit upside the head, maybe. A bunch of insults and commands. A daily reminder that he was good for nothing, a thug, *maldito.* Loser.

He needed money of his own. A job or something. That way he didn't have to go begging his dad for things he wanted.

The guitar he wanted was somewhere under his stomach. He rolled over and found the magazine, then flipped to the page with the pearl-white Stratocaster. There was no way his dad would get it for him.

Down the hall, Alex had started on the third movement. It

was at times delicate, his fingers trickling over the keys, a cascade of notes, building and circling, intertwining with each other, the right hand and the left, a playful and joyful dance.

Julian hated it. He hated every note, every tick of that metronome. He hated that his dad loved it and paid for those lessons, and that all Julian could hope for was a crinkled piece of glossy paper in a magazine. A picture. A stupid picture.

It didn't make him feel any better knowing he'd made Alex cry. It felt good at the time, shoving that toilet seat over his head, but what did that matter now? It meant nothing.

He had to get out. He couldn't take listening to that metronome anymore.

The backyard was hot. The sun was unencumbered by clouds, a fireball hanging in the sky. Maybe Jay would be home, maybe he could get him to open Mr. Ray's pool.

Julian biked down the long driveway to the Rays' house. He hoped that Jay's little sister wasn't around. He didn't know why, but he wanted to avoid her if he could. He couldn't stop thinking about the look on her face when he'd thrown Alex down on the grass the other day. She had hated Julian, sure, but that look she gave Alex? It was worse than hate. It was—

It was like she knew what would come next. The end of things. The scared little *puta* running away from her 'cause he couldn't face her, and Sarah left standing there. Alone.

Why did that matter? He didn't need to think about it. She was Alex's friend, not his. The whole thing was stupid.

Julian rode around the basketball court a couple of times, hoping Jay would see him, but nobody came out of the house. He didn't feel like ringing the doorbell.

Julian decided he didn't want to swim.

When he rode back home, he saw Mr. Henderson puttering around in his garden. The old man seemed older, like skin-and-bones older, his face all sunken and gray, a walking-dead corpse, his bald head spotted with those liver spots all the old people get if they live long enough.

"Hey, Mr. Henderson!" Julian tried to smile. His mom always said it was a good smile. It was kinda crooked, just one corner turned up, one cheek brightening, but she said his eyes were softer when he smiled.

Mi ángel. She used to brush the hair out of his eyes when she said it.

So Julian smiled at the old man, hoping to catch him off guard.

Henderson looked up and glared. Julian hopped off his bike and let it drop onto the grass.

"Mr. Henderson, you need any help around here? Like moving boxes or something? I saw you moving stuff the other day."

"I'm all done with that," Henderson said, words as clipped as one of Alex's arpeggios on the piano.

"Okay, then maybe I mow your lawn? Help in the garden?"

"Certainly not."

"Okay." Julian let the smile drop. "It's just, I need to make a few bucks—"

"'I'm sorry, young man," Henderson said, his face like some kind of ghoul in a cornfield, "but I have no need of your... assistance."

He bent down and went back to the garden. It was flush with ripening tomatoes and wide, leafy cucumber plants, the bounty of the garden bigger than Julian could ever remember seeing before.

"Yeah," Julian said under his breath, "right." *Old bastard.* What was Julian thinking? That asshole wouldn't help. Nobody would.

He picked up his bike and walked it back to his garage. He didn't even bother to lean it against the wall, just let it drop on the concrete floor. Papi would probably break his neck when he got home. *Leaving your shit in the middle of the floor? What the hell is wrong with you?* He could hear his dad already.

Julian brushed past the living room without even a look at Alex. He headed down to the basement, strains of Beethoven accompanying his retreat.

Hours later, the video game screen blinking, telling him to start a new game, Julian sighed and tossed the controller on the floor.

The house upstairs was silent. Maybe Alex had gone over to Sarah's. Julian almost wondered what Jaime was doing, but he stopped himself. He wasn't gonna give Jaime the satisfaction of wondering. Those guys were pussies, anyway. All those guys. Thinking it means something to know what shit goes on under the hood of a car.

The taste of pizza grease was still on his lips. And on his fingertips, the smell of copper and nickel. The number was burned into his brain. He didn't even need the address book to know it. It was there like a tattoo, stamped on the inside of his eyelids, like the after-image of light when you squeeze your eyes shut.

If no one was home, maybe he could pick up the receiver in the kitchen and dial the number and hope he didn't chicken out this time.

Rick's voice had surprised him. It was so different from his dad's voice. Julian had a lot of beef with his dad, but Alejandro Guerrera was no punk. That Rick, though, he sounded like a punk. The kind who got his ass beat in.

How could she? That was the question that ran through his head. Not just because of Rick's voice, but because of everything. Julian didn't want to think of her as his mother anymore. She wasn't worth thinking about.

But maybe he could call the number again.

"HELLO?"

That voice. Like some kind of rat in human form.

"Uh—"

"If this is a solicitor, take me off your list."

"I ain't selling nothing."

"Well then—"

"You Rick?"

"Yes."

"Listen, Rick." Julian's throat felt so dry. *What am I doing? He's not gonna tell me.*

"Who is this?" Rick's voice was starting to rise, the rat-king trying to assert his dominance.

"You don't know me. I'm looking for Maria—"

"Maria?"

That got his attention. "Yeah, Maria," Julian repeated.

"Who's asking?" Suspicion. Rick wasn't a total fool.

"I'm her kid, okay? I gotta talk to her."

There was a fuzzy silence, like when somebody puts a hand over the receiver and all the sound goes muffled. Julian almost hung up the phone, but he stopped himself.

What if she was there?

He'd figured she'd be there, but when that fact was made evident, when that muffled silence meant Rick was talking to his mom on the other end, hiding their voices so Julian couldn't hear, it hit Julian like a slap on the face. His cheek stung from the pain: a bright, hot pain. He clenched his teeth and closed his eyes.

He couldn't open his eyes again, or it would all come pouring out.

"Which son?"

"Huh?"

"Which son are you?" Rick asked. "Maria wants to know."

Which son? Did that make a difference? The seal around his eyelids was starting to strain. He couldn't possibly keep it all in.

"I'm Julian."

"Hang on." There was that muffle again, that veil between him and the grown-ups, that forbidden territory where kids weren't supposed to go. Off-limits. Let the grown-ups talk. Not something you need to hear.

Julian knew it all. All the excuses. Mom and Dad arguing behind the door like they thought nobody heard them, Mom and Dad with ice in their veins, chilling the room so everyone else's blood could freeze too and the two of them could get on with hating each other while the kids ate cereal and pretended not to notice.

That's what that hand over the receiver meant. Julian wasn't supposed to know what the grown-ups were saying. He just had to live with the consequences.

"Mijito." His mom's voice sounded strange. He recognized it, but it was like a woman doing an imitation of his mom. Close but not quite.

"Mami," Julian said, though it came out garbled and way scratchier than he meant it. He couldn't help it when his eyelids leaked. Tears ran down the length of the receiver and made his hand wet.

"I'm so sorry, mijito," his mom said sounding like she was a thousand miles away. She wasn't, of course. She was just with Rick, that rat who worked with her downtown, the two of them holed up in his apartment somewhere.

"Listen, Mom," Julian said, "I don't wanna talk about it. I just… I wanted to know if you could help me out with some money. There's this guitar I want, and Papi won't pay for it. He's being a real asshole about it, and I need a couple hundred bucks. That's all. It can be an early Christmas present or something. If…"

If you were even gonna be around for Christmas.

"Oh." His mom's voice fell flat. "I see."

"You don't have to bring it here," Julian said quickly. He felt her slipping away. A thousand miles became ten thousand. "I can meet you somewhere."

"Oh, mijo." She didn't elaborate, but she didn't have to.

Julian knew. Why did he ever expect anything different? He wasn't the one she'd wanted to talk to. He hung up the phone without another word, then wiped his hand on his t-shirt.

The metronome sat atop the piano, its pendulum pointing an accusatory finger. He swiped—quick, hard, cruel—and knocked it across the room. It hit the floor with a heavy thud, but it didn't break.

He went to his room where the magazines were still piled on his bed. He tore them up, one at a time, two at a time, pages ripped and ripped again, hurled through the air, stomped on and shredded, until images of guitars and rock stars and amplifiers and chords and picks and strings and all the other dreams he had wished for were mutilated and strewn across the carpet.

He was still crying.

Outside, there was no sign of Alex or anybody. Mr.

Henderson was gone. The woods behind the house beckoned, but Julian ignored the summons. He didn't want to go back there. Alex had spoiled his secret place. Invaded it.

The sky was wide open above him, the sun not as high nor as hot as before, but Julian had nowhere to go. He was trapped. The driveway ahead, the driveway behind, he could go in any direction, but they all led the same way: nowhere.

He did what instinct told him to do. He grabbed his bike and took off. If he couldn't have what he wanted, he'd take something else.

THE BOOKSELLER EYED HIM IMMEDIATELY, so Julian didn't hang around the candy display. He wandered down the stacks, glancing at the book spines but not really caring. Maybe the old fatso would go in the back room or something, or a customer would come in and distract him. Julian didn't even want candy, he just wanted to take it.

He craned his neck to see what the bookseller was doing. He was sitting on his stool, hands folded over his immense belly, pretending to sleep. Julian knew the trick. Lull the kids into false security then bust them. The old guy had tried it before. Julian wasn't that stupid, though. He could wait.

When he turned his head away from the bookseller, his eyes couldn't help but see a rush of colors. The books. They popped out at him with their colorful spines: blood-red, and shimmering emerald, and a rich, honeyed gold. The lettering of the titles was ornate, scripted to look like silver lances or brands of fire.

This was that fantasy shit Alex and Sarah were always

playing. Like that game of Jay's that was just a bunch of pencil scratches on paper and some lame dice rolls.

Julian scowled, but he didn't move. He wanted to hate these books, but he couldn't move past them. He found himself almost reaching for one.

"Is the neanderthal even capable of reading?" The bookseller was right next to Julian suddenly, breathing down his neck. He had the smuggest look Julian had ever seen on his sweaty, piggy face.

Julian snatched a book from the shelf. He didn't even bother to look at the title, just turned it over and pretended to study the back cover just to piss off that old fatso.

"Death Wing Cycle, eh?" the bookseller replied. "Not my first choice by any means, but it might interest someone of your sort. There's a mutilated dragon corpse in the second prologue that probably appeals to your diseased mind."

"Sounds lame," Julian said, shoving the book back into its place. "All these books are for weirdos anyway."

The man huffed. "I would expect nothing less from you. Ridicule a thing you cannot understand."

"You don't know jack about me. Just 'cause I don't like your stupid dragon shit doesn't mean I can't read or whatever. It's lame, that's all."

"Ah yes, I forgot," the bookseller put on a mocking smile, "you prefer the pages of *Guitar Land* and nudie magazines."

"What if I do? Some of us care about getting laid someday." Julian pushed past the old man and headed for the exit. He saw the candy display on his right, all the Day-Glo colors and obnoxious advertising trying to entice kids to load up on sugary crap. Julian reached out his fingers and swiped a handful of Radioactive Firebombs. He knew the bookseller was watching.

Let him call the cops. Who cares.

He shoved open the door and the little bell above it twinkled. Julian stopped in the doorway, his foot already standing on the sidewalk out front. He turned. The old guy was still there, standing where he'd left him. He didn't look smug anymore, or even angry. He just stared at Julian, a strange look in his eyes. Then he nodded and walked toward the back room, disappearing around the corner of the stack.

Julian squeezed his fingers around the clear cellophane wrappers on the Firebombs. He could feel the roundness of the hard candies through the crinkle of the wrappers.

He let them fall out of his hand onto the floor. They barely made a sound as they hit the carpet.

Reaching out, he grabbed a guitar magazine. He could see the checkout counter from where he was standing. The bookseller was nowhere in sight.

The magazine's glossy paper felt smooth in his hand. He stood there for an eternity, one foot still on the sidewalk, warm air wafting in and mingling with the air conditioning, the magazine starting to stick to his sweaty palm, his eyes fixed on the checkout counter. All he had to do was leave. There was no one watching.

A moment later, the bell of the door jingled again. Hurried sneakers ran for the parking lot. The overhead door hinge slowly eased the glass door shut.

When the bookseller returned, the boy was gone. Waddling back to his stool behind the counter, he stopped when he saw the money. Three dollars and fifty cents sat on the worn wooden countertop. He swooped it up with deft ease and punched it into the cash register.

The register sang out its song. Another transaction complete.

CHAPTER TWENTY-TWO

Bike Riding

WHEN SHE LOOKED BACK out the window, after turning the last page of the book, Sarah saw the trees framed by an endless sky, like a gentle blue ocean, and the sun an island floating in its midst, not a cloud intruding on that scene, not a single blemish, only a slight breeze that moved soundlessly beyond the glass. Sarah caught her breath and gazed at the trees as they swayed in that gentle rhythm.

Summer was ending.

The bookmark with the unicorn on it was laid carefully atop the stack of books at the foot of the bed. Two copies of *Gates to Illvelion* sat side by side on Sarah's comforter.

The end of the book, the end of August.

Sarah closed her eyes and tried to picture the story one last time. The forest, the quest, the gates and their key, and the queen waiting beyond. It was everything she hoped for. Friends reunited, family restored.

Sarah's chest ached. It *had* been perfect. A perfect story, no matter what Agnes said. If only Sarah could find the words to write a story like that, then perhaps the aching in her heart might be quelled.

But summer was ending, and that brought her little comfort.

Picking up the copy of the book from the Book Depot, Sarah headed out, into the kitchen, past Grandpa playing solitaire at the far end of the table, then out the screen door, past the daddy longlegs that sprawled themselves like wispy stars across the white stucco walls of the house, past Grandma in her garden, picking tomatoes, past the garage and the familiar smell of oil and iron, all the way to where the old bikes leaned against the side of the garage, to where Sarah's bike waited, seat hot in the sun, tires melting into asphalt.

She put the paperback into her back pocket and kicked up the kickstand. The breeze came alive in her ponytail as she rode down the driveway, past the basketball court and the pool. No more visions of faerie knights creeping along the edge of the forest, no more bats flitting above the lawn.

They never did swim in the pool at night anymore, never did taste traces of chlorine on their lips as the darkness swelled above them and the stars shone as bright as fireflies.

Maybe next summer. Maybe someday.

Would anyone swim with her again? Or was that a passing dream?

Sarah rode down the driveway, a tunnel of trees on either side, past the wild woods on her left, past the tangle of woods that enclosed the clay mines, past the young trees on the right, past the paths of the nine queens winding deeper and deeper into the heart of Avalon.

Sarah rode past Alex's house—no one home or no one wanting to be found home—and Sarah turned her face from the house. She stared instead at Mr. Henderson's garden, so full and fruitful with late summer's bounty, and then she saw the FOR SALE sign at the end of his driveway, and the piles of old furniture and empty frames and boxes stuffed with the world's treasures. And Sarah rode past, her eyes casting their sight on the way ahead, trying not to look back. They stung anyway and swelled enough that Sarah had to blink away the tears so she could see.

Still, she rode past.

Down the streets of the subdivision, all the while wondering if the creature was following, if it was loping its way along the edge of the woods, the vast forest tracing a path across the backyards and lawns of every house.

She pedaled harder and only once did she look to see if the creature was there. It was nothing but houses, nothing but trees.

So Sarah rode past and onto the paved trail between the subdivisions, the path leading out to the middle school. Boys were playing baseball on one of the fields. Sarah's bike coasted down the winding path, the sun bearing down on everything, turning up the heat a hundred degrees. The school loomed ahead, a cinderblock fortress, the hot asphalt parking lot a ghost town. A bat cracked and boys cried out, coaches yelling for someone to run for home plate, and Sarah turned and saw it clear as fireworks.

Alex had flung his catcher's mask off and braced for the base runner's collision. He had the ball, he stood his ground, a pile-up at home plate, and still he held on, raising his fist in the air, the white ball a talisman, an offering to the sun and to summer and to victory. The team cheered. A hero was swallowed up by his teammates. Alex was lost in the crowd.

Sarah was glad for him even as she rode past.

She rode past the sweltering parking lot, past the school, past the sign that said WELCOME BACK, and past the darkened doors that would soon open and beckon hoards of children inside. Sarah rode past them all, not yet ready to cede her summer to those doors.

Where would she be in three weeks? Would her mother call and claim her? Would California take them back?

Or would she walk these strange halls and sink into the background of sixth grade, a girl without a friend?

Down the sidewalk, cars from the main road whizzed past, and the shopping center just ahead. Sarah rode past the grocery store and the coin collector shop and all the afternoon old ladies and moms doing their shopping, right to the door of the Book Depot, right to the place where her bike would rest against the store window, taking its ease beside the colorfully painted train on the window glass.

The bell rang and a gust of cold air greeted her. Sarah loved the smell of the bookstore. She breathed in the books, gathered into herself the smell of the paper and the smell of dust, the smell of all those stories just waiting to jump into her head.

The bookseller was shelving a box of books a few rows down. Sarah took the weathered copy of *Gates to Illvelion* out of her back pocket.

"Thank you," she said, handing it to the white-haired man. "It was perfect."

The man raised an eyebrow. "You can keep it, you know. In the world of retail, we call this transaction a 'sale.' Refunds are frowned upon if everything was satisfactory."

"I don't need a refund. I just wanted to give it back."

The man was puzzled, but he took the book from her. "Most unusual."

"I have another copy," Sarah said, smiling.

"Another copy?" The bookseller gaped. "But how? This book is too rare—"

"If I told you, you wouldn't believe me."

Sarah looked past him, not at the books, but at the racks beyond, the back wall and all its bric-a-brac. "Do you have any journals? Like diaries or notebooks?" she said.

The man's eyes narrowed, but he stepped aside to let her pass. "Back corner. Stationary."

"Thanks!"

Sarah bounded past him, the money in her pocket burning a hole since two days ago when her mom had sent it, an early birthday present. Her mom never could get the timing right.

Most of the journals were leather-bound, or faux-leather, in solid colors of turquoise, pink, or brown. They felt smooth under Sarah's hand, thick with blank pages. But she moved past them. They didn't have the magic.

There were diaries, some with flimsy locks and tiny keys, but the cover designs were all trademarked properties: pastel ponies, rainbow-colored bears, strawberry hats, and circle-eared mice. The diaries tempted Sarah, but their cheap keys were a pale comparison to what could really unlock secrets. She would be fooling herself if she thought those flimsy locks could keep anyone out.

She moved past the diaries, past the stationary, past the cards and envelopes, until she found a spinning rack of spiral notebooks, the kind that fit into three-ring binders—the kind you bought for school—and on the top rack was a notebook emblazoned with a white unicorn, its horn glimmering in a moonlit scene, its cloven hoofs riding through a stream in a silvery forest, riding straight toward her, fleeing an enemy or riding to adventure, it didn't matter which, but riding toward her, seeking her out.

Just a spiral notebook, but Sarah held it fast. Already she could see the words streaking across the wide-ruled pages, stories and tales and worlds filling the blankness, the unicorn a messenger and guardian of her dreams.

"School supplies are on discount," the bookseller said as Sarah placed the notebook on the counter.

"It's not for school." She was already taking the money out of her pocket, smoothing out the crumpled bills.

The bookseller closed his eyes and sighed heavily. "It's still on discount," he said through tight lips, "whether you use it for algebra or not."

"It's definitely not for algebra," Sarah replied, grinning. She could hardly say what it was for, but she knew that as soon as there was pen in hand and blank page open, she would have no trouble with words. They would shower the page like starlight falling from the summer sky.

"Indeed," the bookseller said, taking her money and ringing up the sale. He eyed her again, studying the strange look on her face, wondering what mischief she would make.

As she picked up the notebook again, Sarah could feel an electric current tingling her skin, a promise of what was to come.

THE BREEZE outside blew her home. It was stronger now, a heavy wind that almost bent the trees, so Sarah had to pedal hard to fight through it. She squeezed her elbow into her side, desperate to keep the notebook she'd tucked under her arm from slipping. She pedaled past the strip mall and back to the subdivision paths.

As the trees swayed and shook their leaves over the neighborhood, Sarah was already thinking about where she'd go with that notebook. Not her bedroom, not the kitchen table, not even outside in the grass or under a tree. She needed a special place. A magical place.

Her thoughts were so caught up in daydreams that she hardly noticed the woman and man at the edge of a thick patch of trees that bordered two manicured lawns. Sarah only saw it out of the corner of her eye, that vision, and at first, she thought it was a tree stump, or a shrub, or some ordinary thing. She was fighting so hard with the wind that she wasn't thinking of queens or knights or Avalon.

But when she looked again, now on purpose, she saw it as clear as pool water on a cloudless day. A woman sat upon the grass in front of a copse of hemlock, birch, and oak. She wore a long green gown, her head covered in a wimple, and in her lap, she cradled the head of a man, his head uncovered and his eyes gazing up into hers, his body resting on the lawn. The sun was in the western sky, but it shone brightly, and it glinted off the man's chain-linked armor and polished gauntlets, illuminating the image emblazoned on his ivory tunic: a sturdy oak with branches that reached to the sky and green leaves that matched the hue of the woman's dress. The shape of the branches reminded Sarah of the shape of a heart.

The man smiled into the woman's face, and she into his, and the vision was as solid and real as the notebook nestled under Sarah's sweaty arm. The wind swirled, and Sarah had to pedal hard to stay upright, but for the briefest of moments, the woman in green glanced up and nodded to the girl speeding by on the bike, the girl who had stayed true to the magic of Avalon.

But Sarah didn't see. She had already ridden past.

"Dinnertime!" Grandma Ray called as Sarah leaped off her bike and bounded into the kitchen to find a pen. Everyone was outside at the white picnic table, sitting down to barbecue chicken and corn on the cob, their happy voices echoing off the aluminum awning. The grill was still smoking, filling the air with the scent of charcoal. The wind had died down.

Aunt Isabel was next to Uncle Jim, both of them laughing at some private joke, and Jay was already reaching for another drumstick, but Sarah had no time for greasy fingers slick with barbecue.

In the kitchen, she rummaged through the old coffee cup Grandma Ray used for holding pencils and pens and found the ballpoint pen with the most ink in it. The blue cap was lost, but that didn't matter. Sarah had no plans to cap it anytime soon.

She started for her bedroom when Grandma came in to get another pair of tongs.

"Enough fooling around," she said, frowning. "Come and eat."

Sarah stopped mid-gallop, the ballpoint pen tight in her fist, the unicorn notebook still under her arm. Alice Ray's eyes flitted to the shimmering equine on the notebook's cover. Then she saw her granddaughter's face. Sarah's eyes said it all. *Not this time, Grandma. Please. Let me have this.*

Somewhere in the back of her memory, Grandma Ray remembered journeys through the Cretaceous period, through the glaciers of Antarctica, back into the sawdust air of a circus where she rode a pony and dreamed it was Pegasus. She saw her father's ghost standing there behind Sarah.

"Go on," she said, the tongs momentarily forgotten. "I'll keep your food warm."

Sarah sprinted upstairs and dug out the Carolingian coins from her shoebox. They felt heavy in her hand, and she rubbed her thumb over the imprint to feel its texture. She needed to remember these things now, needed to soak them up.

As she exploded through the screen door and back outside, Sarah barely had time to wave at Aunt Isabel's generous smile or answer Grandpa Ray's questions. She ran off down the hill toward the forest. There was only one place she could go.

When she got to the gates, they were still half open. She realized with a laugh that she hadn't shut them last time. The sun was sinking lower, turning the world into that golden hour just before dusk. She sat down beside the gates, dying stalks of wild grass poking into her bare legs. She set the notebook on her lap and rested the two coins on her knee. Then she turned to the first blank page and started to write.

Avalon is ruled by nine queens. They rule it with terrible magic.

She thought for a moment before continuing.

But there are some who would fight them and discover the way to break their enchantments. All they needed were stout hearts and strong swords and two coins to make their wishes come true.

Sarah kept writing until the sun sank faster and faster behind the trees. She wrote all the stories and ideas she had conjured that summer, all the tales and quests, and fallen leaves turned into dragon's blood, and old barns became ancient crypts, and bats flew above black watchtowers, while a dwarven magician studied arcane tomes in amber lamplight.

She wrote about the nine queens, and the lady in green, and the Oak-Hearted Knight and his twin, the Faerie Knight, and she spun new tales too, tales that sprang from wells so deep she didn't know their bottoms. Everything she had ever dreamed of poured out of that blue ballpoint pen and onto the crisp pages of the spiral notebook.

And she wrote about a friend who was lost to her, lost to the enchantments of the world beyond the forest. She mourned for him and their days spent traipsing through the trees, and even though the words were hard to write, she was grateful for them. They helped quell the aching in her heart.

When dusk had settled over the woods, her pen stopped and she knew it was time to leave. There would be other days, after all, other chapters to finish.

And the gates would still be waiting.

Sarah tucked the notebook under her arm, shoved the coins in her pocket, and jogged home. Past tree shadows, and the last waning fireflies of August, and the sweet smell of warm grass, Sarah ran up the hill to the big black and white house, back to her bed and her books, and her family, and her dinner kept warm in the oven.

Summer, 1992 was ending. And Sarah Lewis was ready for the next adventure.

Gates to Illvelion is a real book. It's definitely not the greatest fantasy ever written. Not even close. But it is real.

I would know. I wrote it.

When I was working on *Avalon Summer*, I knew I wanted Sarah to discover a book that would have eerie parallels to her own life. In order to write about it, I figured I needed to know a few things: chapter titles, character names, some plot elements. So I made them up. I started with the chapter titles, then expanded into other details, and before I knew it, I was writing the whole story, turning this plot point from *Avalon Summer* into a real fantasy novel.

I called it *Gates to Illvelion* ("Illvelion" being an alternate spelling of the Arthurian name, "Avalon"), and I worked on it alongside *Avalon Summer*. I never consciously tried to fit the two stories together; I let my unconscious mind do the work of figuring out what kind of story would appeal to ten-year-old Sarah, and I wrote the story that came to me unbidden and unplanned.

The fact that it became a story about a young girl who befriends a boy in the forest while searching for her family was my unconscious mind at work. It knew what Sarah wanted to read, I guess.

Gates to Illvelion is its own distinct work. It looks and feels like one of those old fantasy paperbacks from the 1970s or 1980s, something I myself might have found when scouring the shelves of Waldenbooks. It's not necessary to read *Gates to Illvelion* after reading *Avalon Summer*, but you can if you want.

When I was a kid, I was browsing the fantasy section in the bookstore at the mall, and a strange man, round and white-bearded (like Santa Claus), came up to me and told me if I wanted to read the greatest fantasy ever written, I needed to read T.H. White's *The Once and Future King*. He pointed out the book, and I took it down from the shelf. I still have that old beat-up copy on my bookshelf to this day.

I'm not sure *The Once and Future King* is the greatest fantasy ever written, but I'll never forget that moment in the store. The man was a bit creepy, to be honest, but his recommendation also made me feel like I was part of a secret club, a society of fantasy fiction readers who spoke in reverent whispers about their favorite novels.

As I studied the book cover, I turned to talk to the man again, but he was gone. At ten years old, I was convinced he had vanished into thin air, an apparition from the realms of Faerie sent to guide me to my destiny. He probably just went to the checkout counter, but to my young mind, it was magic.

Who knows? Maybe it was.

Acknowledgments

This book wouldn't be possible without the help of so many people, most especially my husband, Paul, who gave me the encouragement and love I needed to follow my passion; and my children—Natalie, Paul, and Henryk—who stirred my imagination with their own crazy make-believe games, and who were very good about leaving Mom alone while she wrote; and my parents, who supported me not only with free babysitting for the kids but also by backing the Kickstarter that helped fund this project.

To all my Kickstarter backers: Jason Baldwin, Mona Contardi, Jon Jon, Katie Zbytowski Kuznicki, Richard Novak, Joseph Pesci, Michael Pesci, Marcus Skywalker, Katherine Shipman, Maryann Sligay, Dan Vigi, Lea Vigi, and K. York. Thank you for taking a chance on this book! I can't believe how quickly we funded this project, and it was all due to your support.

And thanks especially to my grandparents, Rena and John, who made a house where everyone was welcome. Their home —nicknamed The Forest—was an irreplaceable part of my life and the lives of everyone who knew them. Their door was always open. Their home was my home; I will always miss it. Without my grandparents, this book wouldn't exist. I wish I could've written this story before they died, but at least I can give them this tribute: The Forest lives on, I hope, in these pages.

About the Author

Jennifer M. Baldwin lives with her husband and children in Michigan. She spends most of her days reading dusty old paperbacks, rolling 3d6 down the line, and wishing unicorns were real.